WHEN WE DARE

WILD FIRE SERIES

J.H. CROIX

Copyright © 2025 J.H. Croix

All rights reserved.

Cover design by Najla Qamber Designs

No part of this book may be reproduced in any form or by any electronic or mechanical means, including information storage and retrieval systems, without written permission from the author, except for the use of brief quotations in a book review.

NO AI TRAINING: Without in any way limiting the author's exclusive rights under copyright, any use of this publication (in any and all formats, including ebook, print, audio, translation, and any other formats) to "train" generative artificial intelligence (AI) technologies to generate text is expressly prohibited. The author reserves all rights to license uses of this work for generative AI training and development of machine learning language models.

This is a work of fiction. Names, characters, businesses, places, events and incidents are either the products of the author's imagination or used in a fictitious manner. Any resemblance to actual persons, living or dead, or actual events is purely coincidental.

The mention of any real company and/or product is for literary effect only. Such mentions should not be construed as endorsements or, or from any of these brands. All trademarks and copyrights are the property of their prospective owners.

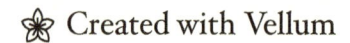

❧ Created with Vellum

To the pets who show us what matters.

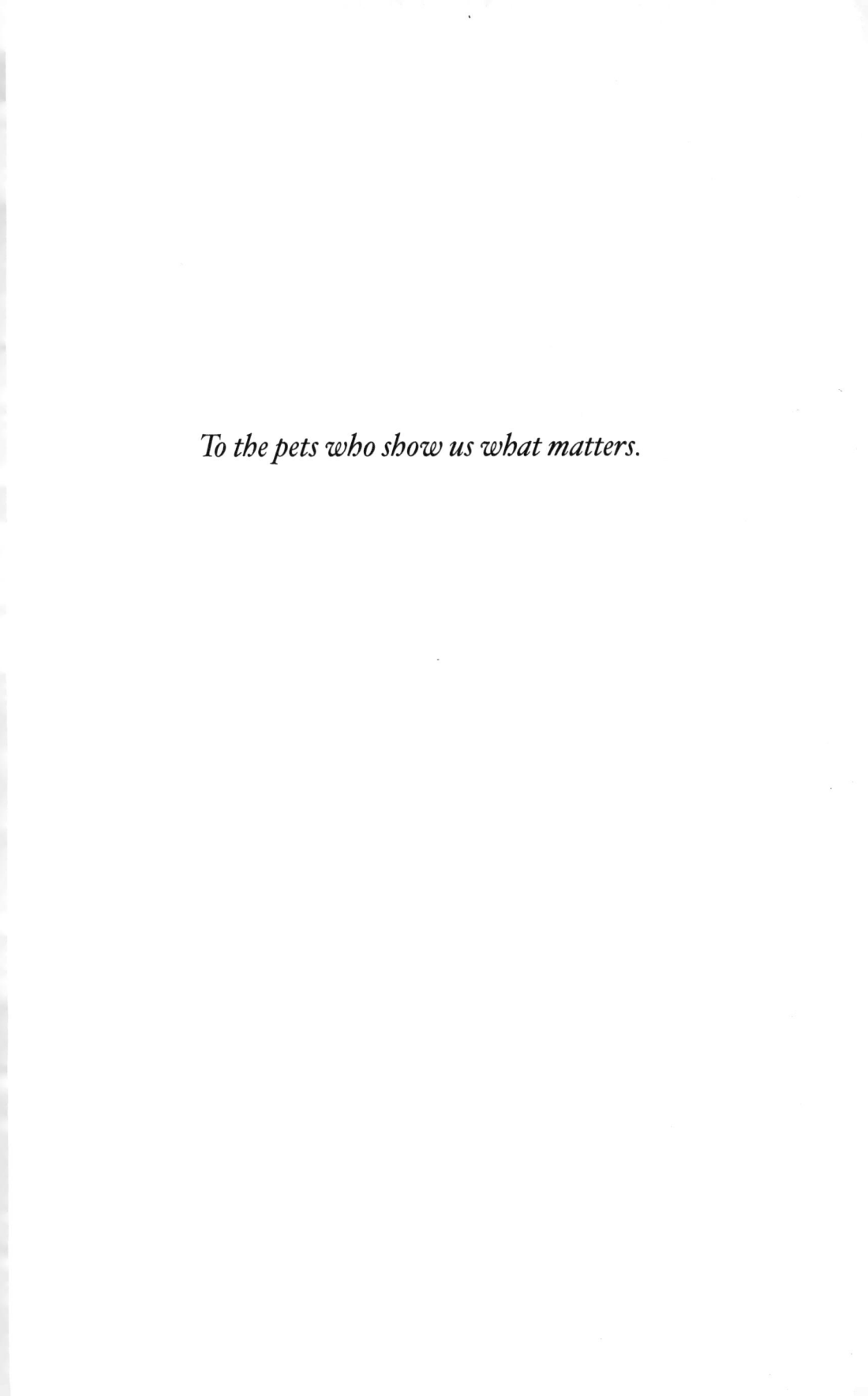

Chapter One
STELLA

Sometime in January

"Trashcan turkey," I said.

Tish eyed me curiously, her brows hitching up. "Trashcan turkey?"

"It's awesome. You put a trashcan on an old broom handle, or something like that, put the turkey on it, and smoke it over charcoal or wood."

"Wow," my friend said.

"You've never heard of it?"

"I can't say that I have," she said dryly.

"I promise it will be delicious," I said.

Tish shrugged, her lips teasing with a smile. "I trust you. Go for it."

Several days later, I walked into the yard at Tish and Griffin's house. I tromped through the snow to where Griffin had told me there was a fire ring. I had an old broom handle I'd scrounged up. Once I tripped over the rocks for the fire ring, I kicked them loose to prop up the broom handle. Griffin had already placed a tidy stack of firewood out here and left a bag of charcoal for me.

In short order, I had a turkey smoking under the trashcan and felt pleased with myself for getting it all set up. My mom used to make turkey like this when I was little and I had fond memories of it.

Tish came out with our mutual friends, Madison and Maisie, to check on the status.

"Oh, wow, this looks like..." Maisie paused, her brown curls bouncing as she glanced my way.

"Trashcan turkey. It's smoked turkey," I explained.

She giggled as Madison eyed the project curiously.

"Look I grew up trashy and poor. I'm living up to my heritage," I pointed out with a shrug.

"You're a paralegal and you just finished law school," Tish pointed out. "That's not trashy."

I snorted as I poked at the fire with a long tree limb I'd found in the snow. "My past is complicated."

"Well, my dad was a card shark and got arrested for it a few times," Maisie offered with a wry smile. "That's why I usually win when we have card night."

I'd heard bits and pieces of Maisie's story, but this detail was news to me. "Seriously? That's why you're so good at cards."

She nodded. "My dad is really good at cards. He still is. He's still a scammer and still trashy."

Since she was laughing about it, I let my own laugh sputter out. "Well, I learned how to make trashcan turkey from my mom who's got a heart of gold, but she's kind of trashy too. Not a card shark though. I wish she had been, maybe we'd have had more than two pennies to rub together."

Madison was eyeing the situation skeptically with her hands on her hips. "My parents were rich criminals," she offered.

"What?!"

"True story," Madison said, her tone dry.

"Learn something new every day," I said, completely unsure how else to respond to that.

Madison grinned. "My point being that money doesn't tell you much about people."

Maisie helped me add some more rocks to help stabilize the stake at the bottom, while Tish and Madison headed back inside.

"It's a campfire in the winter." Maisie bounced in the snow as she smiled at me. Her cheeks were pink from the cold. "If this works, I'm gonna tell Beck we have to do it next year for Thanksgiving."

"I've actually never done it by myself, but it worked when my mom did it."

There were more people than I had expected to be here at the not-a-holiday party Tish and Griffin had organized. I met Tish when I helped handle some of the details of her custody case. When I moved to Willow Brook, Alaska to work in the expansion office for the law practice I'd worked for in Fireweed Harbor, Tish had welcomed me into her circle of friends here.

I was relieved to have a project to keep me distracted because Hudson Fox was here. Ever since I'd driven over one of his crutches months ago, I'd stumbled into the worst crush on the guy. I felt ridiculously flustered around him. Seeing as he was friends with many of my friends, it was difficult to avoid him.

For today, I could focus on my little project, but I was starting to feel like I had overpromised on this. When Tish started planning this, someone requested turkey and this seemed like a fun way to cook it. Even with my mother's instructions, I fretted. I studied the trashcan, which was starting to glow orange.

"There's a fire under it, this is how it's supposed to be," I said out loud to myself.

A raven was watching me from the trees, judging me, or so I thought. "Why are you looking at me?" I asked when it let out a startlingly human-sounding call.

I had no clue if the bird was answering me when it let out another sharp call into the icy winter air. It was roughly twenty feet away in the trees, perched on a bare branch above the snow. A magpie flew by, chattering at the raven who ignored it completely. All things considered, the raven was much larger and gave the magpie just as judgy of a look as it gave me.

The problem with this whole project was I didn't even know how to check to see if the turkey was done. I fretted some more before leaning down to add some lighter fluid to the coals. Mistake.

Next thing I knew, there was a trashcan-shaped ball of fire. I could totally handle this. I looked toward the raven. It stared right back at me, still giving off judgy vibes.

I fetched my fire gloves and ran over, grabbing the trashcan again and flinging it into the snow. Everything was fine. Until my hair caught on fire.

I heard the sound of footsteps hurrying across the back deck. I hoped it was at least one of the firefighters. A moment later, someone lifted me and tossed me into the snow.

My fall was cushioned by at least three feet of snow. "Oh, my God!" My exclamation was muffled by the snow on my face.

I was discombobulated and felt someone's hands sliding over my back and my hair. I was pretty sure it was a man because they were big and strong.

And then… "Stella, what the hell happened? Are you okay?"

Freezing cold and covered in snow, I rolled over and looked up into Hudson's green eyes.

Chapter Two
HUDSON

Stella Lancaster stared back at me. Her big brown eyes were wide and her freckled cheeks flushed pink from the cold and the snow. Her blond curls were damp from the snow with a few singed locks of hair from the fire.

I'd just purposefully thrown her into the snow to put out the flames.

"I'm fine!" She looked annoyed.

"Your hair was on fire along with the back of your coat," I explained.

I was practically lying on top of her. Even through her winter coat, I could feel her curves. I forced myself to roll away from her and sit up in the snow.

She sat up with me and eyed her heavy fireproof

gloves. "My hands aren't burned," she said as she slipped the gloves off.

I glanced toward the deck to see there was a crowd watching. "Is Stella okay?" a voice called over.

A moment later, we were both standing. "I'm fine," Stella insisted again.

"Your jacket is burned in some places on the back," I pointed out. "Your hair is kind of burned on the ends too."

Her lips twisted to the side as she let out a heavy sigh. "I'm pretty sure that caught on fire first." Stella patted her hair and winced slightly.

"Let me see," I said. I stepped around her and carefully brushed her hair away from the back of her neck. There were a few angry red spots and burns. "Your coat kept you safe, but you have some burns above the collar. It's actually—" She moved to pull her jacket away from her neck. "Don't!"

I was too late, and she let out a yelp. Graham, Madison, Tish, and a few others were making their way over through the snow.

"Oh, my God," Stella muttered under her breath. "How bad is it?"

"We should take you to the hospital to get it cleaned."

When she peered up at me, there were tears in her eyes. The adrenaline from the rush of what happened was fading.

"You'll be fine," I assured her, holding her by the shoulders. "You have a burn on the back of your neck and it just needs to be cleaned. Everything else is fine."

She blinked. "How's the turkey?"

Madison reached us. "The turkey looks great." Her gaze shifted to me. "Take her to the hospital and come back."

"I don't want to go to the hospital. It'll take forever," Stella said. She blinked rapidly, trying her damnedest not to cry.

Tish curled an arm over her shoulders. "Just go. With burns, you don't want to worry about infection."

"We're going to wait to eat until Holly can get here anyway," Madison assured her. Stella was keeping it together. Madison hugged her carefully. "I'll trim your hair tonight if you'd like."

Stella let out a little sigh. "Okay."

"I'll drive," I said.

Getting through the jumble of everyone checking on her was like walking a gauntlet, but I herded her through. Madison and Maisie promised her they would finish dealing with the turkey.

Once we were in my truck, Stella sat stiffly in the passenger seat, leaning forward a little.

"The turkey looks amazing," I said.

Stella let out a deep sigh. "I can't believe that happened."

I slid my gaze to her as I turned onto the main road. "It's a story," I offered with a chuckle.

"I hate this kind of drama, and now I have to cut my hair."

"How does your neck feel?" I asked a moment later.

I was paying attention to the road, but I heard the tears in Stella's voice. "It hurts a little."

I glanced over to see her swiping her fingers over her cheeks.

"Hey, it'll be okay. They just need to get it cleaned up."

"I know." Her swallow was audible. "I just feel so stupid and it stings. I don't want to take pain medicine either. I hate it."

"They'll probably put some numbing gel on it when they clean it. You should be good to go with regular ibuprofen. You can always do that trick where you alternate with acetaminophen if it hurts too much."

She took a shaky breath and dragged her sleeve across her face when I glanced over again.

I wasn't thinking when I reached over for her hand. She looked a little startled, but she curled her hand into mine as I gave it a squeeze. "You'll be fine."

"I know." She cast me a small smile and my heart gave an unsteady kick.

A few minutes later, I ushered Stella into the

emergency room. Holly Fox, my cousin's wife, happened to be at the desk. "Hey, what's going on?" Holly asked instantly.

Stella turned around and lifted her hair up. Holly's eyes widened. "What happened?"

"I was making trashcan turkey for the party, and the trashcan got too hot and my hair caught on fire," Stella explained. "Hudson saved me by throwing me in the snow."

When I met Holly's face, her lips were twitching at the corners. "Good job, Hudson."

Stella rolled her eyes. "You can laugh."

Holly smiled warmly at her. "I'm just glad you're okay."

"Your timing is perfect, things are quiet. Let's get you back there and get that burn cleaned up. You wait," she ordered me.

Chapter Three
STELLA

I was relieved Holly was at the ER. I really liked her. She was sharp and a little bossy. I'd met her through Tish.

"Just a sec, I'm about to use some numbing spray," Holly said. "It'll feel cool and then you won't feel much. If you're worried about the burn, it's not so bad. The main thing is to keep it clean."

The tension eased in my shoulders as the numbing spray did its job. I could feel her briskly cleaning the back of my neck. Needing a distraction, I asked, "Is Nate a firefighter?" With Willow Brook the hub for four hotshot crews, there were firefighters aplenty. Holly's husband was often with many of the other firefighters I'd met around town.

Holly snorted. "Nate's a pilot, but I understand why you'd ask. There are a lot of firefighters around, too many. Nate has a contract with the state to ferry them out to fires. That's not the only flying he does, but it sure keeps him busy during the summer."

I could feel her carefully placing a bandage over the area she'd just cleaned. "You're all set. I'm not a hairdresser, but do you want me to trim away the burnt ends?"

"How bad does it look?"

Another nurse came into the room. Holly ran her fingers through my hair, holding it to the side for me to see. "Just a few singed ends." She glanced toward the other nurse. "I was asking if she wanted me to trim them off."

The nurse smiled, her eyes warm. "I'll help. I used to cut my kids' hair."

"Go for it."

Moments later, they said I was good to go after the doctor on duty cleared me. It really didn't take that long at all. Holly waved me off and assured me she'd see me in a little while.

Hudson was waiting in the lobby. When I saw him, my belly flipped over and my pulse rocketed. With his rumpled brown hair and intense green gaze, it was almost hard to look into his eyes.

"How you doing?" he asked when I stopped in front of him.

"Fine." My breath felt a little shaky.

It felt weird to have him here. I didn't have any

family here to wait for me. I ignored the achy twist of my heart at that train of thought.

"Ready to go have some trashcan turkey?" he asked lightly.

I couldn't speak, so I just nodded. When we reached his truck, he held the door for me. As I started to climb in, I turned around abruptly, startled that he was right there. But, of course, he was. "Thank you!" I blurted.

"Of course." His eyes coasted over my face.

I swallowed, trying to gather my wits. "You hardly know me, but you made sure I didn't get burned worse than I could've because I was kind of panicking. Then, you took me here, so... Just, thank you."

He stared into my eyes. For a split second, I felt a powerful pull toward him, almost visceral. I had to check myself. I could feel my body leaning in his direction.

"No problem," he finally said, his voice a little gruff.

My hand was curled on the inside door handle, and my breath was a little short while my pulse galloped along. Flustered, I turned, bumping into him with enough force that I lost my balance. Hudson steadied me, one of his hands landing on my hip.

"Take it easy," he said.

My pulse went wild all over again. By some miracle, I got into the passenger seat. When he started driving, I felt like the space around us was lit with a charge.

I got busy telling myself to get it together. I didn't need to be having the hots for Hudson. Relationships were a terrible idea for me. I couldn't even manage something casual because I ended up feeling desperate, desperate for someone, anyone, to commit. It never worked out.

A therapist had explained to me that my relationship patterns were a form of repetition compulsion. I was compulsively drawn to men who were similar to the men my mom dated. In short, unreliable and flaky. My nervous system recognized them. I was drawn to the familiar and unconsciously kept hoping it would turn out differently.

This fiery chemistry with Hudson was a sure sign I should stay far away. That way lay the abyss of emotional desperation, of falling in love too fast when I didn't even know what love was.

When he pulled to a stop at Tish's house, I practically ran like I was on fire to get inside and avoid him.

Chapter Four
HUDSON

That evening, I tried to keep my focus on my friends. It shouldn't have been that challenging. Except every time I looked toward Stella and her blond curls bounced around her shoulders, and her dimples peeked out when she smiled, and her cheeks turned pink, my body felt like an engine revving.

When I left, I happened to be walking out behind Stella. I paused beside Stella's car because I couldn't help but check with her. "How are you feeling?"

She looked up at me, something flickering in her eyes. "You were right. Ibuprofen is enough. I'm fine." She lifted a hand, shifting her fingers through her curls. "And, I have shorter hair now." Her smile was sheepish.

Fuck me. The urge to kiss her was nearly strong enough that I acted on it. I barely managed to keep myself in check.

"Thank you for, uh…" She paused, her nose wrinkling adorably. "Rescuing me and taking me to the hospital."

I had to clear my throat to speak. "Anytime. Just glad you're okay."

I drove away, telling myself it was best to keep my distance from Stella.

Hell, she was a lawyer. If she knew about my past, she would run for the hills.

———

"Hudson!" Maisie said when I came walking through the back hallway while holding a tray of coffees aloft.

"You're just happy to see me because I'm delivering," I teased as I carefully checked the coffees in the tray before handing her the one with her name written on it.

"Maisie's always happy to see us," Griffin said as he rested his elbows on the counter encircling her desk.

"So, is he Huddy Hudson or something like that in your phone?" Rex Masters teased as he straightened from behind the desk, where he was putting away some files.

"Hudsy," Maisie said, her brown curls bouncing with her nod.

"Hudsy? Excuse me?" I prompted.

Rex chuckled. He was the police chief in Willow Brook and also Cade Masters' father, a firefighter here. They looked remarkably alike, although Rex had more silver in his brown hair and deep laugh lines around his green eyes. "Maisie gives everyone nicknames in her contacts. I'm Rexy Rex."

"I'm Griffy Griff," Griffin offered with a wry grin. "The only one who gets something different is Beck. What is he again?"

"Action hero," Maisie replied with a dimpled smile.

Beck happened to be coming out of the hallway and chuckled as he heard her reply. He leaned across the desk to give Maisie a kiss on the cheek. "I love my nickname. I *am* an action hero."

I chuckled as I rolled my eyes. "So, I'm Hudsy Hudson?"

Maisie nodded. "Can't be inconsistent, or somebody will feel left out."

"Sweetheart, I'm pretty sure nobody will feel left out," Beck offered.

"I appreciate the consistency," I teased.

Rex waggled his brows as he slipped out from behind the counter and headed toward the police side of the station.

Just then, the door to the reception area opened

and we collectively glanced over. As soon as my eyes landed on the man walking in, I was so startled that my mouth dropped open.

"Hudson Fox! Holy fucking shit!" Parker Grayson exclaimed.

I met my old friend halfway across the waiting area and pulled him into a backslapping hug. When I stepped back, I asked, "Wow, what the hell are you doing here?"

Graham came walking into the waiting area. "He's joining our crew. How do you two know each other?"

I didn't hide my past, but I didn't broadcast it either. Things had been rough when I was younger, and I'd ended up with a juvenile criminal record. Parker and I had met in detention. I'd walked the straight and narrow ever since.

I could see the questions in Parker's eyes, and I had my own for him. Glancing to Graham, I replied, "We knew each other back in high school. We were both raising some hell then."

Parker held his hands up. "I'm winning at living the most boring life since then," he said dryly.

"Same." I held my palm up to slap him a high-five.

Maybe plenty of people got in trouble in high school, but not all of them got nailed for dealing drugs with their dad like me. Parker ended up in detention for the same reason. We'd bonded pretty tight for those months and had stayed in touch sporadically since.

"Good to see you, man. I'm glad you're going to be on the crew." I meant it. Parker was solid. Maybe it was strange if you'd never done any time in detention, but you saw people's true colors there. When everything was stripped away, maybe the only thing you had was finding your dignity and being honest.

Maisie was all business, fetching some paperwork and handing it over to Parker before she took a dispatch call. The group filtered apart, and I walked into the back with Parker and Graham.

"It's really good to see you," I said when we stopped in the locker area.

"You too." Parker's brown eyes crinkled at the corners with his smile. "I wasn't expecting to see you, but I'm damn glad you're here."

"We've got plenty to catch up on," I replied with a chuckle. "Aside from work, what brings you to Willow Brook?"

"That's it. I've heard good things about Willow Brook, so I jumped on it when I saw they were moving a crew here."

"Good move. It's a great area. I was about to go work out." I thumbed over my shoulder toward the workout area in the back.

Parker was putting his gear in the locker Graham

had directed him to. "Carry on, man. I've gotta take care of this paperwork."

I clapped him on the shoulder before leaving the locker room. I lifted weights and settled in for some time on the elliptical. My mind spun back to my days with Parker. My dad wasn't the most stable guy. He'd made his money running drugs from Seattle up to Alaska and he'd roped me into it. I was too young to know better. When I got in trouble, I'd lucked out with a good public defender. He'd whittled my sealed record down to a few misdemeanors. I wasn't ashamed of my past. I still felt like a dumbass sometimes. I had turned thirty this year and it had been almost fifteen years since I walked out of detention. After that, I'd scrambled to stay out of trouble. I loved my dad, but he'd stayed busy doing dumb shit until the last few years. I had no memories of my mother. All I knew was she didn't stick around. I was doing all right and counted my blessings every day.

After I finished working out, we went out on a training exercise. On the drive home, I ordered a pizza for delivery. I'd scored a nice rental through a fellow firefighter, Russell. He had a duplex with a shared kitchen on a pretty lake. So far, the upstairs part of the duplex had stayed empty, although Russell had told me the other day that someone would be moving in soon.

Not long after I got home, I jogged up the stairs when the doorbell rang, assuming it was my pizza delivery. But when I answered, my mouth dropped open.

"Stella?"

Chapter Five
STELLA

"Hudson? Um, what are you doing here?" I sputtered.

"I live here in the unit downstairs. I thought you were the pizza delivery guy," he replied.

I stared up at Hudson, my hormones spinning cartwheels inside, while my pulse bolted as if it was trying to win a race.

"What are you doing here?" he asked while I remained speechless.

"Um, I guess I'm your neighbor now, or about to be. Phoebe told me about this rental. Upstairs, I think?" My voice sounded squeaky and I hated it. I cleared my throat. "I guess Russell and Paisley own this place, and..." I pointed up to the sky for some reason.

"They do."

I stood there, uncertain what else to say. "Have you seen it yet?" Hudson finally asked.

"Paisley texted me some photos. I know her and so I just went for it." I cleared my throat again. "Will it be okay if I'm your neighbor?"

Hudson's eyes widened. "Of course. It's a duplex, but there's a shared kitchen. I think it was originally built to be a vacation rental."

The sound of tires on gravel came from behind. I spun around, relieved at the distraction. The delivery guy jogged out and handed Hudson the pizza. A moment later, after Hudson paid him and waved him off, he opened the door wider. "Come on in. Nobody else has been here since I've been living here. I haven't been in town that long. Maybe about six months. You can go on upstairs. I actually haven't been up there at all.

"Here's the shared kitchen," he said as he led me in, gesturing ahead.

My hormones thought this whole thing was freaking great. Maybe we'd see Hudson more. Me and my hormones were *not* friends. They had bad judgment.

Hudson showed me the kitchen, which was just beyond the entryway. It was open and bright with lots of counter space and a view of the lake.

"You can have some pizza if you want," Hudson offered. He got two plates out of the cabinet.

"Um, sure. I'll just go upstairs and see what it looks like."

I hurried out of the kitchen, fumbling with the keys before jogging up the stairs. When I crested the top stair, the space opened up. The stairs came into the center of the living area. One side had a couch with a TV mounted on the wall, and the other had a desk and some shelving. To one side at the back of the stairs was an inviting bedroom with a big bed and a bathroom with a rainfall showerhead centered over a soaking tub.

Paisley had explained to me that she and Russell had updated the space before they moved out with the plan to rent it. Like the kitchen downstairs, the living room offered a beautiful view of the lake. It was early evening and close to dark with lingering colors from the setting sun shimmering on the water and the moon rising through the violet sky.

"You can handle Hudson living downstairs," I whispered to myself. "He'll be gone a lot in the summer anyway."

I'd been making do in a small garage apartment that Tish had helped me find, but it wasn't a great option long-term. It was too tiny.

Steeling myself, I took a deep breath and hurried back down the stairs. Hudson was already chowing down on pizza. Of course, the man was sexy even when he was eating. He wore a T-shirt, the soft fabric caressing his muscled chest and shoulders lovingly. His sweatpants rested low on his hips. His bare feet were hooked around the rungs of the stool.

My hormones sat up and took another long look. I resolved to remember that my hormones were idiots and they could have their feelings, but *I* would be sensible. I'd been sensible for years now. I hadn't been on a date in over five years at this point.

I tended to go for guys who wanted it all from day one. All meaning sex. They wanted that when all I wanted was love and safety.

"I'm sure it's nice up there," Hudson said.

"It's really nice."

"The only reason the upstairs one wasn't available when I moved in was Paisley and Russell still had a bunch of stuff stored there. My understanding is the layout is like my place downstairs. Help yourself." He gestured to the empty plate on the counter across from him.

I was legitimately starving, so I sat down across from him and tried not to notice he was even sexy when he chewed. To make matters worse, he had ordered pepperoni pizza.

"My favorite pizza," I admitted.

Hudson nodded somberly, as if this was a really important detail. "Good. I can trust you then."

I burst out laughing. My heart did a little cartwheel while my belly spun in flips when he chuckled and his green eyes twinkled.

"Are you moving in tonight?" he asked.

"Probably tomorrow. I wanted to stop by before I showed up with all my stuff."

"I'm around. If you let me know when, I'll help you move."

That was the neighborly thing to do, so I told myself. "I'll give you my number," he added. "Just text me."

Chapter Six
STELLA

The following day

"Mom, what are you talking about?" I'd lost track of my earbuds and had my phone jammed against my shoulder as I threw the last few things into some boxes.

"You have a half-brother," she said. "You know this."

I had to clench my teeth to keep my sigh from escaping. "Mom, I don't know this."

I didn't point out that, of course, I'd suspected it. My mom had boyfriends by the bushel when I was growing up. My life had been chaotic and unsettled growing up with her. We'd barely scraped by financially. She'd pinned her hopes on finding the right guy to bail her out and was always desperate for love. My sperm donor had been around some when I was a baby, but I didn't remember him. My mom told me he bounced in and out of jail on minor charges, so she hadn't tried too hard to stay in touch. She insisted he had a heart of gold, if only he could straighten his life out. That was basically her in a nutshell. She was loving and kind and a hot mess.

I'd always suspected I had unknown siblings out there.

My mom carried on. "Your dad has a son. I have no clue where his mom is. He tracked me down because he's looking for you. I told him that you're in Willow Brook and you're a lawyer." I could hear the pride in my mom's voice.

My heart twisted because I *knew* she was proud of me. I was proud of me. After witnessing her stress and worry about money throughout my childhood, I'd become determined to be able to take care of myself without relying on any man. Ever.

"How do you even know if this is a real thing?" I asked.

"I hear about your dad on occasion, so I called him up and asked. I didn't tell him why I was asking though, so he doesn't know about the connection yet." It was totally on brand for my mom to call someone out of the blue and ask if they had a child.

"He's no longer a pharmaceutical rep." That was what my mother called his former work, if you will, as a drug dealer, which was hysterical, but whatever. I let that slide. "He's going to meet me for lunch soon. While maybe your dad hasn't been the most involved, he was always a good guy at heart."

"Please tell me you didn't give anyone my number." I wasn't ready for an unknown brother that I'd never met to want something from me.

"I didn't! I promise."

"How did he find you?" I asked.

"He did a DNA test. That's how he found me. Remember, we did that thing a couple of years ago and I manage your account so it's my email listed with your results?"

"Oh, yeah. But if my dad had a son, how come he didn't just hear about me from his dad?"

"Because he had your brother first, but he didn't know about him when he was with me. Your brother's mom never told him until he got a call when she took off. By that point, your dad and I had broken up and I was trying to stay out of trouble, since he was definitely not making the best choices for a while there," she explained.

I silently sighed. "Okay, well, I'm not sure what to do with all of this."

"I just wanted you to know. I've got his number. He was very respectful. He said he understood that you might not know he existed and that this might be weird. His name is Parker Grayson. He's a firefighter. I'm so excited to reconnect with your dad too! Maybe it will be special."

If I counted sighs and almost-sighs when it came to conversations with my mother, at this point, I was in the millions. And yet, I credited her with so much. People taught you many things in life. Despite her struggles, my mom was ever-optimistic and loving. Maybe she was flaky, but I never doubted her love for me. She'd also taught me what I didn't want to be. I never wanted to be desperate. I never wanted to look for one man after another to try to make my life work.

"I love you, Mom. We'll talk more about this, but I have to go. I'm in the middle of packing." I *did* have to go, but I also just didn't want to be on the phone for that much longer. My mom tended to evoke a whirling sense of anxiety sometimes.

It wasn't her, but rather all the old worries and anxiety from when I was little. Worries that something would change too fast, that something else would fall apart, and that her own nearly chronic anxiety would grip me. She would be devastated at the end of every relationship, and I felt her pain like my own when I was little.

I understood why, or I thought I did. Her childhood had been filled with uncertainty. She thought having a baby would make it all better. She'd loved me in all the right ways. But all those boyfriends had been exhausting. Once, she had found a real creep and that resulted in a child protective services report. Fortunately, my mom was protective and as soon as she realized what was going on, she'd kicked that guy out of our lives and we'd both started therapy.

My therapist, even though I only saw her for a little while before we moved, had been awesome. She had helped me learn how to manage my own anxiety, to pay attention to what I could and couldn't control. It helped a lot, but anxiety was an asshole and still made lots of noise in my own thoughts.

"I'll text you Parker's number. If you decide you want to reach out to him, you can do that," my mom said.

"I will think about it," I replied. I knew my curiosity would eventually get the best of me, but I needed time to let this news percolate.

"I love you, sweetie!"

"I love you too, Mom."

After the call, I doggedly kept packing. If it had been anyone's life other than mine, maybe I would've been a little shocked to discover I had a brother out there. But I'd always known it was possible. Loving though my mom was, her judgment in men wasn't stellar, not even close. Once I was old enough to understand, she'd never misled me about who she thought my bio-father was, but she'd made it clear he hadn't been around since I was a toddler.

My mom was pretty flawed, but then I suppose everyone was. Her love was fierce. Even though my childhood had been unstable and we'd always been rubbing pennies together to get by, I wouldn't have traded her for a second.

As promised, she texted my newfound brother's phone number. She also shared a screenshot from a text he'd sent her after they connected.

Please let your daughter know I understand this might be awkward. I don't have much family, so I'm trying to find whoever I can.

I saved Parker's number. Maybe he was a good guy. Maybe he could be somebody else to count on in my life. My mom had always been there for me when I needed something, anything at all, but we only had each other.

Not much later, I tucked the last box into the back of my small car and bumped my hip against the door to close it.

I'd contemplated calling my brother later. For now, I had to get through moving into my new place and telling my hormones to chill the hell out around Hudson.

A short drive later, my heart was doing jumping jacks in my chest and my belly felt all tingly as I looked up at Hudson. He easily lifted the last box out of my car, and my eyes trailed along the flex of muscles in his shoulders as I followed him up the stairs.

I was going to have a stern conversation with my hormones.

Chapter Seven
HUDSON

After I set the last box on the floor against the wall, where Stella directed me, I turned to face her, resting my hands on my hips. "Anything else to carry?" I asked.

Stella stared up at me. Her brown eyes were wide. She blinked before her tongue darted out to slide across her bottom lip.

Fuck me. Stella was too freaking cute. A revving sensation sizzled through my body. I was going to have to get a grip. At the moment, I was wearing a T-shirt and sweatpants. It would not be cool for her to notice my cock was at half-mast.

She cleared her throat but didn't say anything.

"Stella?" I prompted.

"Oh! That was the last box."

"Is that all you have?" I couldn't help but ask. I'd helped her carry maybe eight boxes inside. "If you need me to follow you back to your place with my truck, I'm happy to help," I offered.

Her curls swung as she shook her head. "That's it. I don't have a lot of stuff."

We happened to be standing by the wall with a waist-high wall on the other side flanking the staircase that came into the center of the main room. Because Stella had asked me to stack the boxes against the other wall, there wasn't much space. She began to turn and her foot caught on the edge of a box.

She let out a soft, "Oof!" when she stumbled.

I reflexively reached for her. Her momentum flung her against me. She was a lush bundle of softness when she bumped into my chest. Her cheeks went pink and her eyes wide.

Holy hell. She felt *so* fucking good. In the muddle when she tripped, my hand landed just above the curve of her bottom. She was fully pressed against me. I could even feel the taut little peaks of her nipples.

Without a doubt, I knew she could also feel the swell of my cock. The thread of my control was almost to its breaking point.

I couldn't seem to move, and the moment stretched like elastic between us. My eyes dropped to her mouth, noticing that her lips were parted and her breath was coming in soft heaves. Her tongue darted out again, sliding in slow motion across her bottom lip. Her lips were fucking perfect. When she smiled, it was a little lopsided with one dimple peeking out first. The flush on her cheeks deepened.

"Stella..." I heard myself rasp. My fingers pressed into the sweet curve of her bottom, and I couldn't help but bring her a little closer.

"Hudson..." she whispered, the throaty sound of her voice like a jolt of lightning sizzling through me.

I sucked in a breath, scrambling for some kind of sanity. "Can I kiss you?"

The part of my mind that could still think, that was still slightly rational, was absolutely positive she would tell me to back the hell off. Kissing her before was reckless, but now she lived upstairs.

She didn't say anything. I felt her lean closer just before the hot shock of her lips met mine. It was like a clap of thunder followed by lightning, an electric jolt to my entire system. I groaned and slid a hand into her hair as I fit my mouth over hers.

Stella made this little sound in the back of her throat that nearly brought me to my knees. When she pressed herself even closer, I felt one of her hands slip around my back. I kissed her as if my life depended on it. Her tongue slipped out, gliding against mine.

I had no idea how long we kissed. All I knew was I was hard and hot. The length of me was swollen to the point of pain by the time we broke apart and stared at each other.

Chapter Eight
STELLA

It was dark when I woke up. I was disoriented. Rolling my head to the side, my eyes landed on a small clock on the table beside the bed. It was four-thirty a.m.

I had to physically shake my head to remember I was in my new apartment. As soon as my brain rewound to last night, my cheeks burned hot in the darkness.

That kiss. With Hudson. Sweet hell. What was I going to do? I shouldn't have kissed him.

"You already did," I whispered in the darkness.

I knew I had a problem when I was speaking to myself in the darkness, alone in my new bedroom. Restless, I rolled onto my side, adjusting the pillow under the curve of my neck. Even the bedroom had an amazing view here. I could see the stars twinkling in the sky above the lake outside.

My thoughts replayed those moments with Hudson. My hormones had gone a little crazy with him carrying my boxes upstairs. He'd been so nice and helpful. He was ridiculously sexy with a rugged handsomeness to him. I'd cataloged the sharp cut of his jaw and the straight blade of his nose in those seconds. I'd wanted to kiss him so fiercely I couldn't stop myself.

I let out a flustered sigh. Just thinking about it, and I was getting all hot and bothered. I was alone, all by myself in my bed. I shifted my legs, letting out a little whimper when I felt the slick moisture there.

I wanted Hudson, so very much. Nothing more than a mental replay, and I started getting wound up.

Maybe he's really nice, my heart chirped.

Sometimes my heart felt like a baby bird, vulnerable, without feathers to protect it and constantly chirping at me. That's how I was emotionally. I knew this about myself. I didn't need to want things from a man, any man.

I sighed again and rolled restlessly onto my back, staring up at the ceiling. There was nothing to see, just darkness and a blank surface. My mind was naughty and disobedient. Every time I told myself to forget about it, my thoughts looped back to Hudson. The feel of his lips molding over mine, the way he took control of our kiss.

"Oh, my God," I whispered to myself.

His tongue glided in to tease with mine. The way he rocked his hips and I could feel his hard length nestling just above the apex of my thighs. I'd been so wet by the time I managed to gather my wits that I didn't even remember how I kept myself in check. I'd walked him down the stairs. All along, my pulse had been galloping madly.

Blessedly, my mom had called me and the sound of my phone ringing upstairs galvanized me. I'd choked out a goodbye and slammed the door as I dashed up the stairs. I never even answered the phone and sat at the top of my stairs, trying to pull myself together.

When I recalled the feel of his eyes boring into mine, my pussy clenched. My hand, disobeying me, slipped into my panties, teasing into my dripping wet folds. This was how bad I had it for Hudson. My fingers grazed my swollen clit. I was hot and wet, so desperate for more.

It only took minutes before I was burying my fingers into myself, the friction from the heel of my hand over my clit spiraling my pleasure into the stratosphere. I was trembling and shuddering, Hudson's name a ragged whisper crossing my lips.

The following morning, I blushed in the shower just thinking about what I'd done. I endeavored to get a freaking grip. Hudson lived here. It was sort of a duplex, but we had a shared kitchen. I wasn't so sure it was a good idea for me to live here. And yet, I was already here and I loved the apartment. It was the best apartment I'd ever had.

After I toweled off, I studied myself in the mirror. My blond curls were damp and my freckles stood out on my cheeks.

"You can handle this," I told myself in the mirror.

I was back to talking to myself. What the everloving fuck?

Blessedly, there was no sign of Hudson when I made my way downstairs to the kitchen. His truck was gone. I made a quick list on my phone of groceries to get on my way home today before leaving.

A few minutes later, I was waiting in my car while a moose and two yearlings ambled across the road in front of me. One of the yearlings stopped and nosed the hood of my car.

Once the coast was clear, I made my way downtown, smiling at the sign for Firehouse Café. The bell jingled as I walked into the café. A second later, I collided with someone.

"Oh! I'm sorry!" I stepped back and looked up into Hudson's green gaze.

Chapter Nine
HUDSON

Staring down into Stella's wide eyes, my brain scrambled. For a split second, I forgot we were in public. I forgot everything but the feel of her soft curves bumping against me.

"Hudson." Griffin's voice broke through my brief distraction.

I spun around just as Stella stepped back, exclaiming again, "Sorry!"

"Yeah?" I glanced toward Griffin.

"You're up." He gestured toward Janet who was waiting behind the counter with a smile.

"Oh, I'll take a house coffee."

Janet said something to the woman standing beside her. I'd never seen her before. Her hair was pulled back in a high ponytail. She smiled at me.

"I'm training today, and I can totally handle a house coffee."

Janet chuckled. "You can handle a lot more than that." She glanced from me to Griffin. "This is Casey. She just started today, so be nice to her."

"I've got a hell of an order," Griffin replied. "Aside from Hudson, I have a whole text for the orders from the station. It's either stressful, or a great learning experience," he quipped.

Casey smiled. "A great learning experience!"

Griffin gestured to Stella, who was in line with us. "Put Stella's on there too."

"Oh, you don't have to get my coffee," Stella said. Her cheeks were pink, and she was studiously *not* looking at me.

"I'm getting over ten coffee drinks, so adding yours to the mix is no big deal. Tish would be offended if I didn't get your coffee for you," Griffin replied.

Stella laughed softly. "Okay, I'll return the favor and get Tish something next time."

"Stella likes it sweet," Janet chimed in.

"I do. I'll go with the vanilla caramel latte today, but make it strong. I don't do that silly skinny stuff though. That's ridiculous," Stella said, lifting her chin.

Janet grinned. "We don't serve the skinny stuff."

"You really don't?" I couldn't help but ask.

"I really don't," Janet said firmly. "I refuse to engage in our society's obsession with weight." She turned her attention to Casey. "You start with these two, and then what's your list?" Her gaze arced to Griffin.

Griffin slipped his phone out of his pocket. "Buckle up." He recited an entire list that Janet jotted down on a scrap of paper.

Casey began prepping our coffees and talking with Stella, who happened to be closest to her. "Are you new to town?" Stella asked.

"Actually, I am. Just moved here. I'm a Southern girl, and I always wanted to come to Alaska. Bucket list." She made an invisible checkmark in the air. "Here I am. So far, I love it. It's beautiful and I have a cute little apartment next door. Janet rented it to me and gave me a job." Casey's smile was warm when she glanced toward Janet.

"I needed to rent the apartment and I had an opening here. It worked out great," Janet said.

At that moment, Holly came walking into the café with Nate. Her sharp gaze bounced from me to Stella. In seconds, she was reminding Stella that card night was tonight, whatever that was.

Griffin caught my eye. "Tish loves card night. She goes whenever she can."

Holly glanced toward Griffin. "Make sure to remind Tish. It's tonight."

A few minutes later, Stella and Holly left together. It felt as if there was a magnet in my body. I wanted to follow her so badly, but I knew there was no slick way to handle this. I kept wondering just how much she regretted our kiss. I didn't regret it, yet I knew it was complicated. I let out a quick breath.

"What's up?" Griffin asked from my side.

"Oh nothing, just thinking about things I've gotta get caught up on."

Griffin's gaze sharpened for a beat, but he didn't press.

That evening, I was walking out of the station, and Nate was waiting beside my truck, his elbow resting on the tailgate.

"Hey, what's up?" I stopped beside him.

My cousin flashed a smile. "Hey, hey. Thought maybe I could hitch a ride with you."

"Of course. Not that I mind giving you a ride at all, but where is your truck?"

"In the shop. Routine maintenance. Easier to leave it for the night than worry about working around it. Holly told me I had to find my own way home because she's with her friends tonight."

"Oh right, that card night thing. Where are you headed?"

"Let's go to Wildlands. We can catch dinner," he replied.

"Works for me. Hop in."

A short drive later, I parked behind Wildlands Lodge & Restaurant.

It was situated in the center of town on a lake. It was a popular tourist destination during the warmer months and also a favorite for locals. When I was a kid, I remembered coming here for burgers with Nate and his parents.

After we stepped out, I turned to look at the lake. "Wow, the sky is putting on a show."

Above the lake, the northern lights were flickering in the sky, mostly green tonight mingled with streaks of blue. The colors were shimmering like a translucent curtain in the sky.

Nate and I walked toward the lake. Our footsteps crunched on the frozen gravel in the parking lot. We stared up at the sky together.

"Never gets old," Nate said after a moment of quiet.

"Definitely not." My voice was low and reverent.

After my jumbled childhood and the churning anxiety I carried from it, the outdoors was almost like a cathedral for me. A sense of peace crowded out the cacophony of anxiety and uncertainty that took hold sometimes.

I drew in a slow breath, appreciating that Nate was comfortable with silence in these moments. After a few minutes, we turned together and walked inside. As usual, the place was hopping.

Nate and I threaded our way through the crowd, joining a group of friends at a large round table in a back corner.

"Hey there," Graham said, clapping me on the shoulder as I sat down beside him.

Nate took another chair and I glanced around as greetings were lobbed across the table. Graham, Russell, Cooper, and Wes were here from my crew. While Beck, Ward, and Remy were here from the other hotshot crews. Just as a waitress arrived to get our orders, Parker approached with Donovan.

"Hey, man," I called, lifting my hand in a wave.

A few more chairs were tugged over from nearby tables and Parker sat down near me with Donovan. Parker smiled uncertainly as he looked around the table. Donovan introduced him to everybody he hadn't met yet.

"Both of you used to live in Fireweed Harbor, right?" Griffin prompted as the conversation carried along.

"I lived there a few times, but not full-time," I offered. "Parker and I knew each other in high school."

That was the truth, but I just left out the fact that we attended high school classes together while we were in detention. While I didn't hide my troubles in high school, it wasn't easy to explain in a large group.

Parker nodded along. "I'm glad our paths crossed

again," he offered. "Can't imagine somebody I would trust more out in the field."

I smiled over at him. "Same goes for you." After our food and drinks arrived, I asked, "How have you been this last decade or so?"

He finished a bite from his burger before pausing, his gaze considering. "Good. Haven't had a lick of trouble in my life since my younger days. Moved out of state for a while. Mostly, I needed to clear my head and get some distance from my dad, you know?"

"I definitely understand that. Sounds like we've kind of followed a similar path with different geography. I've stayed out of trouble since those days. Still get pissed off about how our dads dragged us into that mess, but I'm glad I'm okay now. I'm really glad to see you."

Parker's eyes crinkled at the corners, his lopsided smile familiar.

"So what's the deal with your sister? I didn't know you had a sister."

Although you could bond when you were in juvenile detention together, there were a lot of things you didn't talk about, unspoken rules about family and things. So maybe he had a sister all along and wanted to protect her. I didn't really know.

"I always heard rumors that I might have siblings out in the world. My dad kind of got around, if you know what I mean," he offered dryly.

I chuckled. "I do know what you mean."

"I decided to do one of those you know DNA tests. Lo and behold, my dad had a few connections. I reached out to the mom of my half-sister and she was really nice. She told me about my sister. I don't know if my sister even wants to know if I exist, but turns out she's here in Willow Brook. I didn't know that until after I took the job here. I'm kind of hoping I can connect. Be nice to have another relative," he said with a shrug.

I studied him for a few beats and took a pull from my beer. "I bet that'd be nice for you. My dad was... Well, you know what my dad was like. He's still kind of a flake although he hasn't been in jail for a few years and finally found some legal ways to pay the bills."

Nate stopped by the table, clapping me on the shoulder. "This is my cousin, Nate." I thumbed toward him.

Nate waggled his brows. "That I am." His gaze shifted toward Parker. "Do you have family in town?"

Parker paused before replying, "Maybe, but I don't know yet."

Nate's eyes narrowed, but he didn't press. "Family is what you make it."

Just then, Nate's phone chimed and he slipped it out of his pocket. "Oh, I've gotta take this." He winked before he turned away.

When I glanced back at Parker, he looked thoughtful. "I remember you talking about Nate."

I nodded. "He's from the stable part of my family."

Parker chuckled, and I added, "I'm glad you're here. If your sister *is* in town, I hope you connect."

"I'm trying *real* hard not to have any expectations."

Chapter Ten

STELLA

"You have a long-lost brother?!" Tiffany exclaimed.

"I think so," I said, a little surprised at her enthusiasm.

While I knew Tiffany, I'd only been in town for a few months, so it wasn't like we were besties. Friendships brought insecurity screeching loudly in my doubts. Fireweed Harbor was the closest thing I had to a hometown because we'd lived there the most when I was growing up, but we'd moved around a lot. It felt like I'd always been the nervous new girl. Even though I gave myself little pep talks all the time, it wasn't easy. I tried to believe in myself and scrounge up the easy confidence I was convinced others felt. I desperately wanted friends.

This move to Willow Brook had opened an unexpected door into a circle of women who had friendships. They all seemed nice and were welcoming. I just hoped none of them could tell how anxious I was to have friends, to feel like I belonged.

Hallie pushed her glasses up on her nose as she cast a warm smile toward Tiffany. "She's enthusiastic about it because when she and her brother did a DNA test, Chase discovered he had an entire group of seven siblings."

"It was a big deal," Tiffany said as she nodded vigorously. "And amazing. I love this for you! Have you met your brother yet?"

Tiffany was definitely a heart-on-her-sleeve kind of woman. She'd hugged me the first time we met. I wished I could be as brave and vulnerable as her.

I took a quick breath. "Not yet. I just found out from my mom the other day. I love her, but she's not the most stable mom." This wasn't a big secret in my life. I wasn't trying to bash her, but it was my life.

Tiffany's gaze sobered. "Well, that's another thing we have in common. My mom was a fucking nightmare." She swallowed and breathed in slowly, almost as if she were trying to calm herself down. "I wouldn't go so far as to say I was glad my mom died, but it was a relief."

My heart squeezed tight. I knew I would miss my mother terribly when she wasn't here.

"I'm so sorry. My mom is—" I let out a gusting sigh. "She spent my entire childhood trying to find the right man who would make her life better. She wasn't a nightmare, but that meant we moved around a lot. I attended eleven schools growing up."

Maisie caught my gaze, her eyes widening. "That's a lot. My mom passed away when I was young and I loved her, but my dad was a total flake. The only useful thing he did was teach me to play cards. I would've traded that for stability in a hot second."

"My mom is loving and means well, but she had a radar for jerks. I'm not shocked to learn I have a half-brother, but I don't know what to expect." I glanced toward Tiffany. "So everything went well when you found your brother's other family?"

Tiffany's nose wrinkled. "Everything's good now. It was a little awkward because my bio-dad isn't Chase's bio-dad. For our dad, it didn't change a thing emotionally, but it was kind of a hit for Chase because he adores our dad. Chase got over that hump and got to meet his siblings. Our mom had a fling with his bio-dad before he got married. All in all, it's worked out. Griffin is Chase's half-brother." She thumbed toward Tish who was sitting at an angle across from me.

Tish nodded and explained, "Griffin's family went through some stuff when they were younger, but doesn't every family?"

"Where do things stand with this brother? If you have a DNA test, I'm assuming you know it's a sure thing?" Tiffany prompted.

"According to my mom, it's a sure thing. Long story short, my bio-dad had my brother before me, but he didn't know about him. She stayed away from my dad because he had some legal trouble. All that to say, my brother's name is Parker. He got my mother's number from the DNA place because she listed it because that's the kind of thing she does and she manages my account." I paused, pressing my lips together. "I plan to reach out to him. I just don't know when."

Tiffany smiled softly, reaching over to curl her hand over mine and squeeze. Her eyes were bright with tears. "Call him. It could be amazing."

I swallowed through the thickness in my throat. "Maybe, but what if it isn't?"

Despite her emotional excitement over this situation, Tiffany nodded sagely. "Maybe it will, maybe it won't. Expectations can make things complicated. Try to see how it goes. If you want an emotional support person, I will be there for you."

"Are you an emotional support person?" Lucy teased.

Tiffany shrugged as she grinned. "Yes. I think I'd be good at that. I don't want to be anybody's therapist, but I love supporting people."

Later that night as I drove home, I pondered Tiffany's offer. I'd been putting this idea of a brother out of my mind because it felt like too much to deal with. I didn't want to let somebody down. I was so accustomed to life just being me and my mom against the world.

As I turned onto the road that led to the duplex, I slowed down. The northern lights were putting on a little show tonight, shimmering in the darkness. No matter how many times I saw them, they always took my breath away. But then, Alaska had a habit of doing that with breath-stealing beauty and wildlife aplenty. It helped anchor me in a world where I often felt adrift.

When I pulled into the driveway and saw Hudson's vehicle there, my heart began to gallop in my chest, kicking along faster and faster. I'd been trying so very hard not to think too much about that kiss. I turned off my car, took a deep breath, and had a little chat with my hormones.

Calm the fuck down. I know how it goes when I let you call the shots. I make stupid decisions.

I tried to be stern. My hormones were little chatterboxes, so excited at the possibility that I might see Hudson.

I hurried up the steps a moment later, slipping in quietly. After I closed the door, I peered around furtively. I hoped the next time I saw him, he would be an ass and my brain could be stronger than my hormones.

There was a pair of boots in the tray by the door and a jacket hung on the hooks above. I presumed that meant Hudson was home, but there was no sign of him on the central floor. The kitchen lights were out. I couldn't help but walk through to look at the view from there. Green and blue were shimmering on the lake from the northern lights above. I stepped through the door onto the deck, inhaling the crisp, icy-cold air.

"Wow," I breathed in as I rested my hand on the railing. Northern lights usually looked like a rippling translucent curtain in the sky. Tonight, the colors were mostly green with bright blue flickering here and there along with streaks of silver. It was so beautiful that I forgot to be anxious about Hudson.

After a few minutes, I went back inside and nearly came out of my skin when Hudson said, "Beautiful lights tonight, huh?"

"Oh, my God!" I yelped as I spun around. My palm flew to my chest where I could feel the pounding of my heart.

"Didn't mean to scare you," he said.

Still trying to catch my breath, I muttered, "Well, you did."

He held both hands up. "I come in peace. I was just coming up to grab some water."

He fetched a glass out of the cabinet and

dropped some ice cubes in it before filling it with water. "The water is filtered here by the way, so no need to waste money on bottled water," he offered before he took a swallow.

I was just standing there, stuck in place. I thought I needed some ice, anything, to quell the heat rising like a fire burning out of control inside. My mind, suddenly feeble, tried to beat back the force. I took a quick breath. I heard myself swallowing and the sound was loud in the quiet kitchen.

"Are you okay?" Hudson asked.

I tried to get some more air, but my lungs weren't cooperating. All I could get was the tiniest sip of air.

His eyes narrowed in concern. "It's the kiss, isn't it?" he asked, setting his glass down on the counter as he took a few steps closer to me.

I was still rooted in place beside the kitchen island.

I shook my head quickly. "Oh, no!" I wanted to play it cool. As if I hadn't been obsessing about that kiss every second that my mind wasn't otherwise occupied. As if I hadn't come in the darkness with his name on my lips.

"Maybe we should talk about that," he added next.

I felt my eyes go wide as I shook my head wildly this time, so hard that my curls bounced against my cheeks.

"It's no big deal. Maybe we should pretend like it never happened," he offered.

This time, my mouth got ahead of my brain. "Well, it *did* happen."

His lips quirked at the corners. "It did."

I wanted to slip into his thoughts and see if he was as desperate for me as I was for him.

"I don't do relationships!" I practically shouted.

For fuck's sake, shut up.

Hudson cocked his head to the side, his eyes narrowing curiously. "Ok-aaaay," he said slowly. "I don't either. Why are you telling me this?"

My heart was pounding so hard I could hear the rush of every beat in my ears. "I don't know!" I internally winced, feeling embarrassment mingle with the pounding beat of desire drumming through my body.

I couldn't seem to say anything without practically shouting. I tried to will my hormones to stop clapping and cheering as if we were at a game.

"We could..." Hudson began. He took a step closer, his words trailing off.

My breath became even shorter as my pulse sped faster. "We could, what?" I whispered.

My rational mind had thrown up a flag of surrender to my hormones.

Chapter Eleven
STELLA

Hudson's eyes bored into mine with heat shooting up flares in his gaze. He took another step closer. He was now inches away from me. It felt as if I had a magnet slapped to the center of my chest, pulling me closer and closer. My pulse nearly gave out from the breakneck pace.

I didn't know who leaned closer first, but in a fiery hot second, my lips were a whisper away from his.

"This," he rasped just as I felt the brush of his lips over mine.

I whimpered when he drew away. I was locked in the beam of his gaze as he lifted a hand, his knuckles dragging over the side of my neck, his touch a burning path.

"What do you want?" he asked.

"Kiss me." Although my voice was raspy, the words were strong and definitive.

"Okay," he whispered as he dipped his head again.

The last syllable of that single word was imprinted on my lips before he angled his head to the side and claimed my mouth.

It was a good thing there was a counter right beside me. Otherwise, my knees would've buckled and I would've collapsed against him. Hudson's commanding kiss was everything I needed. He turned me and pressed me back so my hips bumped into the counter. His hand slid into my hair as he devoured my mouth with deep sweeps of his tongue.

I heard the whimper in my throat, the answering low groan in his. I didn't know what it was about Hudson, but the moment we were touching, any reserves I had were stripped away. Everything just felt *right*.

I was accustomed to my hormones making a racket about some guy. Usually, once the kissing began, doubts crowded my mind and I became insecure and uncertain. That was precisely why I was still a virgin because, invariably, I backed out. To be honest, I was annoyed with that detail at this point. I didn't place any value on my virginity. But, now, it loomed large in my thoughts whenever I kissed anyone.

With Hudson, there were no doubts. I was convinced he had to be the best kisser in the universe. If there were medals for kissing, he would win them all.

He alternated with intense, deep kisses before pulling back and dropping hot kisses at the corners of my mouth. When he gentled our kiss again and lifted his head, we stared at each other.

Need was rampaging like a wild storm through my body. My panties were drenched, and my nipples were tight to the point of pain.

Somewhere along the way, Hudson's palm had slid up under my sweater. I could feel the heat of it splayed against my lower back with his fingers curving over the top of my bottom.

When I moved my legs restlessly, he said, "Tell me how wet you are, sweetheart."

Oh. My. God. I was shocked at his bluntness. It felt so dirty. I had to shift my legs again, unconsciously attempting to relieve the intense ache building there.

With his gaze on me, I was surprised when I answered, "Very."

His eyes darkened as he rocked his hips slightly. I couldn't even believe this was happening. My insecurities weren't clanging loudly in my thoughts, crowding out desire.

I felt his thumb slide across my collarbone, the touch subtle and fiery hot.

I didn't know what to do with how I felt. All I

knew was I didn't want this to end. When I shifted on my feet again, Hudson's hands dropped to my hips. He turned me around.

"Do you trust me?" he asked. Every word he spoke was a soft rasp.

"Yes," I whispered.

My sweater had ridden up around my waist and the counter was cool against my belly. I was still wearing my skirt from work, which was maybe ridiculous, but I liked to dress nicely. It was a holdover from never having the chance to do that often when I was younger. Even though it was winter, my thighs were bare because the skirt came all the way down to the tops of my boots.

Hudson's hands smoothed down the sides of my hips, and I felt one curling around the hem of my skirt followed by the brush of his knuckles as he dragged my skirt up.

"Oh, I like these hearts," he murmured.

My panties were pink with white hearts scattered all over them. If this had been anyone other than Hudson, I would've felt a little self-conscious. With him, I didn't. He draped my skirt just at the top of my waist. I had to bite my lip to keep from moaning when I felt his fingers drag over wet cotton between my thighs.

He teased me with subtle touches until I broke, whispering, "Please..."

"Can I touch you?" he asked.

"Yes..." I gasped.

It felt like forever before he pushed the cotton to the side and teased his fingers into my folds. I was dripping, so wet for him. I almost came the instant he sank one finger inside of me. I whimpered, pushing my bottom back.

A second finger joined the first, and he began pumping in and out of me slowly. I had never felt like this before. Oh, I had plenty of orgasms. I had an excellent vibrator.

Yet, this intense need for someone else to be present for my pleasure unfurling was intoxicating. He fucked me slowly with his fingers, stretching me a little bit. He reached around to the front with his other hand. My clit was so swollen I could feel it pushing out. He teased around it with the flat of his fingers.

"Please...hurry..." My words came out in broken pants.

I was whimpering and begging. When he sank his fingers inside once more and gave me just a little more pressure over my clit, I cried out sharply, shuddering all over as my fingers flexed against the counter. The surface of the counter was cool against my cheek when I turned my head to the side, resting there as I tried to catch my breath.

Hudson was quiet for a moment before he slowly withdrew his fingers, carefully put my panties back into place, and pulled my skirt back down over my hips. Another moment later, he helped me straighten and turn.

I didn't know what I expected when I finally gathered the courage to look into his eyes, but it wasn't the shocked look there. We stared at each other. While I felt raw and stripped bare from having him bring me to a climax so swiftly, he looked simply stunned.

"Are you okay?" I asked, genuinely wondering.

His throat worked as he swallowed before saying, "Yes."

I wanted more. Right then and there.

Somehow, I knew he wasn't ready for that.

Chapter Twelve
HUDSON

A few days later

Are you okay? Stella had asked, her gaze searching mine.

I was absolutely not okay.

I'd known since I laid eyes on Stella that she was cute. But this wasn't about cute. She'd tossed a little silk lasso around my heart and cinched it tight.

All this time, I was trying to convince myself it was just a little extra chemistry, to give it time and it would fade.

I had plenty of reasons why I avoided romance.

I was still relieved I'd somehow gotten my life on a good path after my disaster of adolescence. My good angels liked to believe that if it hadn't been for my father, I never would've gotten in trouble in high school. While that was partially true, I also knew there was a darker side. The little devil on my shoulder had enjoyed the fun of it, of trying to get away with things, of trying to bend the rules. All it had taken was a good dose of fuck-around and find-out and I'd never wanted to bend the rules since.

I'd spent most of my life since then wondering if I was worthy of someone, whether I could be good to someone. Aside from his questionable choices in life, my father had been loving to me. But he was a serious flake when it came to relationships. He was charming and handsome and women flocked to him. Over the years, he'd had plenty of girlfriends who thought they could change him. Spoiler alert: No one ever had.

I kept things casual. Not because I wanted to screw anyone over, but because I didn't want to let anyone down.

As my thoughts spun back to Stella with her rumpled blond curls, her freckled cheeks, her big brown eyes, and the way her pussy felt—slick, wet, and clenching around my fingers—I thumped my head against the wall of the shower. My cock swelled just thinking about her.

I turned the water to cold. Even then, I had to take matters into my own hands, literally. This was round three of me coming with thoughts of Stella. She'd become so much more than a fantasy. I knew the sounds she made, I knew the way she trembled when her body quickened, and I knew how it felt when she came all over my fingers.

And, now she was my roommate. All I had to do was walk up the stairs to her room. In the middle of winter, the chances of me finding another place to stay were slim. Finding a good place to rent in Willow Brook was not easy to begin with. It was a tourist destination so many rentals were slated as short-term.

Something about last night with Stella had burrowed into me. The ribbons cast around my heart were strong. Stella could break me and she didn't even know it.

After several minutes under the icy water, I was wide awake and freezing cold. As I toweled off, I made a decision. I didn't like admitting it to myself, but I'd been avoiding her.

I would be direct and tell her I wanted her. Because I did. Holy hell, I wanted her. Maybe I needed to run straight at it, like I did a fire in the wilderness. I also needed to strategize lines of defense around my heart. That meant getting her out of my system. Just like a fire in a dry forest, it had to burn itself out. The more I dwelled on her, the hotter the fire would burn.

I tugged a T-shirt on and jogged upstairs into the kitchen. Stella was standing by the counter, filling a mug with coffee.

"Good morning," I said, my voice coming out forcefully.

Stella spun around. The smattering of light freckles on her cheeks stood out in the early morning light. She looked fresh and pretty. My heart pinched a little. As I stared at her, I realized it had been a grave mistake to avoid her. Seeing her after too many days was a jolt to my nerves.

"Good morning." She took a swallow of coffee.

My eyes were drawn to the way her lips parted just before they closed around the edge of the mug. When she lowered it and slid her tongue across her bottom lip, my knees almost buckled. Need sank its claws into me, twisting tightly.

I cleared my throat. "Do you have a minute?"

Her curls bounced a little with her nod.

I barreled ahead. "Here's the thing, I don't want to get into all the reasons why, but I can't get serious with someone. I realize we've—" I paused when pink flared on her cheeks.

"I guess what I'm saying is maybe we could be friends with a little bit more." As soon as I said that, I felt ridiculous. What the hell was I thinking? Stella was worth so much more than that.

She studied me, curling both hands around her mug. "Okay," she said, startling me.

I'd braced myself for her to be insulted, maybe even upset with me. In contrast, she seemed calm about the whole thing, almost practical.

"I have my own reasons for not wanting to get serious. I don't even want to feel like I need to explain them. It seems like we have some..." Her composure flagged and she paused, biting her lip.

"Chemistry," I offered helpfully.

She blinked and nodded. "I should tell you something though."

"What's that?"

"Not because it matters, but I'm a virgin."

Chapter Thirteen
HUDSON

Four days later

I stood in the shower, ice-cold water beating down over me. Again. I was still in shock from Stella's announcement. It changed everything.

Or, maybe it didn't.

I didn't even know what I was supposed to do with the detail that she was a virgin, except come to terms with the fact that maybe it ruled out having something casual. We managed not to encounter each other at all over the following three days. I told myself it was by chance on her part.

Work was busy because it always was. *Is your work schedule really that busy in the winter?* My cynical mind taunted me.

On occasion, we did go out of town for fires in the winter, but there weren't many to deal with here in Alaska. The town crew handled most of the local calls unless something required multiple crews. Our crew wasn't even on duty right now. Some were out of town, some were keeping a light schedule, and others, including me, were working out, doing training exercises, and so on.

"Fuck," I muttered before turning off the water and stepping out of the shower.

As I got dressed, my mind looped back to Stella. Ever since our first kiss, it always circled back to her.

I didn't want to care that she was a virgin, but I had so many questions. She had already brought me to my knees inside. What I wanted to be uncomplicated now felt complicated. Not just because she told me she was a virgin, but because that detail poured gasoline on the fire burning inside.

Distracted, I forgot to check to see if her car was gone before walking upstairs. When I walked into the kitchen, she turned around, her eyes widening when she saw me. Her cheeks flushed pink within a split second. Our eyes connected, and it felt as if there was an electrical current snapping and crackling in the air between us.

I cleared my throat and stuffed my hands in my pockets. "Good morning," I managed to say.

While I was contemplating what to say next, Stella twisted her hands together, her brow furrowing as she looked over at me. "I probably shouldn't have said anything about that. I just wasn't thinking—" She let out a sigh before chewing on her bottom lip. "It's not a big deal. Me being a virgin, I mean. It's just I get really anxious. I'm not saving myself or anything. Sex never goes well for me. You don't seem like an asshole and so I was just making sure you knew the whole situation—" She stopped and shook her head sharply before adding, "I just made it worse. I'm really sorry. How about we pretend that we never kissed, that nothing else happened, and that I never told you that?"

"I'm glad you told me," I said after a few beats of silence. "I try not to be an asshole." I paused, attempting to formulate my thoughts into something sensible. "I can't forget any of it." Silence stretched like elastic between us. "What do you want?" I finally asked.

Stella's eyes went wide. She stared at me for so long, I started to get nervous.

"Well, to be perfectly honest, I'd like to not be a virgin anymore. I don't think I'm officially a virgin. Because, I mean, I have a vibrator," she added.

My mouth dropped open, and her cheeks went fire-engine red.

Chapter Fourteen
STELLA

Hudson's eyes were wide, and my cheeks were so hot I worried my face might melt.

So, a few days ago, you told this guy you were a virgin, and now you just told him you think maybe not because you have a vibrator. Way to go.

My critical mind was good at its job. I had plenty of practice with beating myself up.

Mentally scrambling, I stared up at him, wishing I could run away, preferably to dive into a vat of ice water to cool myself off. I couldn't think of any way to backtrack from this. I'd spent three days avoiding him and wishing my mouth didn't get ahead of my brain. True to form, my mouth had gone and done it all over again.

"Um..." I began. Brilliant start. "I shouldn't have said that."

Obvious much? Critical me lobbed that into the mental churn of sheer embarrassment.

I finally groaned. "How about we forget I ever said anything? We never kissed, you have no idea I'm a virgin, and you definitely don't know that I have a vibrator," I babbled.

I could feel the burn of Hudson's stare. There wasn't much I could do to make this *more* embarrassing, so I told myself I could handle this.

"I can't forget any of that." His words were slow and deliberate.

I felt as if I were picking my way through a minefield of anxiety and embarrassment and the most awkward series of moments I had ever encountered. And, of course, it was all made worse by the fact that we lived in the same house and I couldn't avoid him.

"If you worked at it, maybe you could?" I pressed.

Hudson's eyes crinkled at the corners as he let out a disbelieving laugh. He didn't seem to be mocking me, more laughing at himself.

"I could try, but it would require some kind of memory-wiping device." His tone was dry as tumbleweed.

My own laugh bubbled up. As soon as it started, the momentum built until it was a full belly laugh and tears were rolling down my cheeks. By the time I pulled myself together, Hudson was shaking his head slowly. I was hot and tingly all over.

The laughter was good because it relieved the pressure of sheer mortification. I sighed and wiped the tears off my cheeks. "I'm sorry to make this all so awkward, but I suppose that's my brand."

"Your brand?"

I shrugged. "You know, like what you're known for. I'm known for being socially awkward, never being cool."

Hudson studied me for several beats. "You're pretty cool."

I rolled my eyes. "I'm definitely not cool, Hudson. I'm almost thirty and I'm a virgin. And, it's not because I'm saving myself for someone amazing. At least, that would make sense. It's because I'm awkward and tense and I can't relax. I promised myself I wouldn't keep dating assholes. That's my other brand, dating assholes, that is. I hope you're not an asshole. I'm not saying that we're dating, because we're definitely not, but we kissed and I tend to kiss guys who are assholes."

I didn't know how to read Hudson's gaze. He was quiet long enough after I spoke that I got nervous. My nerves led to more babbling. "I shouldn't have said anything, I'm really sorry, I don't know what I was thinking. Please, could you just forget all of this? You stay downstairs, I'll stay upstairs, and the kitchen will be like Switzerland. It'll be totally neutral and we'll treat each other like friendly strangers." I twisted my hands together.

"Friendly strangers?"

I felt my curls bounce as I nodded way too enthusiastically. "Yeah, friendly strangers." I thrust my hand out as if to shake his. As if *that* made any sense.

His eyes dropped to my hand. In slow motion, he reached out, his palm engulfing mine. His touch was warm and dry. Instead of shaking my hand, he held it for several rushing beats of my heart. His thumb began to move in slow strokes along the oversensitive skin on the inside of my wrist. I felt as if I were falling, my belly swooped, and my breath became short.

Hudson took a step closer, his eyes darkening, and never once breaking away from mine. "I don't want to forget any of it, Stella. I don't want to be friendly strangers. I know what it feels like to kiss you. I know what it feels like when you come all over my fingers."

I swallowed, barely able to breathe as heat pooled like molten lava in my belly. I couldn't even speak.

"We've established that neither one of us wants anything serious. You said you want to deal with your..." He paused, looking uncertain.

"Virginity," I offered helpfully.

What the hell are you doing?! My mind screeched.

"This doesn't have to be complicated. I think

you already know it'll be good with us. I know I do. We can establish some ground rules."

I felt my head bobbing up and down. *Everything* with Hudson felt good. Even just standing here with his thumb brushing in idle strokes on my wrist. That little strip of skin was on fire with flames radiating outward.

"What do you mean by ground rules?" I managed.

"Well, we already both don't want things to get complicated. You can change your mind at any point and shut it down completely. And maybe, we can't forget what happened, but I can respect any boundary you set. We can just be friends. Even though neither one of us wants to get serious, we should decide if we're exclusive for the purposes of this."

"What's this?" I rasped over the pounding beat of my heart.

"Kisses, making you come all over my fingers and maybe more, but not with anyone else. Do you want that?"

My lungs were pretty useless, but I sucked in enough air to speak. "Okay."

"Okay, what?"

"Let's do that."

"How about you think about it for a few days?"

Chapter Fifteen
STELLA

Hudson's question boomeranged around my thoughts over the following days. I wasn't sure if he was going out of his way to avoid encountering me in the kitchen at the house, but our paths didn't cross. As the minutes and hours ticked by, my nerves felt stretched to their breaking point. I felt restless and impulsive. My hormones had already made their vote perfectly clear. They didn't understand why I was waiting.

He said to give it a few days. I found myself wondering what his definition of *a few* was. I considered three to be a few, but I knew that wasn't iron-clad.

Blessedly, I was very busy with work and studying. I had finished all of my coursework for law school and had thrown myself into studying for the bar exam. I knew I could pass it, but this was the most important exam I would ever take. Meanwhile, things at the office were as busy as ever, offering an escape from obsessing over Hudson.

Late one evening, I was doing a last check of my email to make sure I had taken care of everything for the day when my cell phone pinged with a text.

Tish: *We're meeting for dinner at Wildlands. Meet us there!*

Before I could text to reply, another text came zooming in.

Tish: *It's me, Phoebe, Maisie, Jasmine, and Tiffany so far.*

Me: *I'll be there!*

A mere ten minutes later, I parked behind Wildlands Lodge & Restaurant, facing the lake behind the place. The early sunsets of winter in Alaska were stunners and tonight was no exception. The sky was deep violet with a pink glow shimmering on the snow-capped mountains in the distance. I'd spent all of my life in Alaska between several towns in the Southeastern part of the state, near Fairbanks, and even a short stay up in Barrow near the Arctic Circle. They were all beautiful areas, but Willow Brook just might've been my favorite.

Wildlands Lodge was probably the biggest tourist destination in town. It was a full-scale hotel and a starting point for many outdoor and touristy expeditions. Like most places in Alaska, it also catered to locals. The restaurant was one of the favorites in town. They also had local music and an excellent selection of food.

The moon was rising to one side with the fading colors from the sunset glimmering on the frozen lake ahead. I stopped at the front of my car and took a deep breath, savoring the crisp air. An owl hooted somewhere nearby with another answering in the trees. I looped my purse over my shoulder and began to walk inside. Out of the corner of my eye, I saw motion to the side and glanced over to see a moose with two yearlings following her. They were far enough away that I wasn't too concerned, but I definitely kept my eye on them. Moose were unpredictable and nearsighted. The moose disappeared into the trees just as I reached the door to the back entrance.

"Good night, moose!" I called softly. That was an old habit from childhood. My mom had always taught me to say good morning and good night to animals when we saw them.

I walked down the hallway, weaving through a few other people coming out of the restaurant. The large restaurant had a strong Alaskan vibe with wide-plank hardwood flooring, wooden beams crisscrossing the ceiling, booths lining the walls, and tables scattered about. The kitchen was central with the restaurant on one side and a bar and dance area on the other. Without any music tonight, those tables were filled with overflow from the bar.

After a quick glance around the space, I spied Tish waving from a table in the corner and made my way through the crowd.

"Hey!" Tish curled her arm around my shoulder, giving me a quick squeeze as I sat down beside her.

There was a chorus of greetings, and I slipped out of my jacket, draping it over the back of my chair.

"We're sharing a bottle of wine. If you want something else, I'm sure the waitress will be here any minute," Tish offered.

"I'm driving, so I can't drink more than maybe a half glass. I'll stick with water," I replied.

"We even ordered appetizers," Maisie said, gesturing toward the center of the table.

I was close to starving. I tended to forget to eat when I was working. "This is perfect! I don't even have to think," I said as I reached for a small plate.

I was gradually getting to know the group of friends Tish had connected me with, but I still stayed mostly quiet. I was new in town. Old habits die seriously hard and all that. With my life of bouncing around from school to school when I was younger, I usually felt like the new kid. Once again, I was the new kid here in Willow Brook.

Tish was sharing an update on her son's leaps and bounds in growing through babyhood. "When they're born and you can't sleep for months on end, you think it will never change. Next thing you know, they're crawling and you're racing to catch up."

Amelia grinned over at her. "I know, it's wild. Pretty soon, I'm gonna have to figure out school schedules, and I'll be posting memes about waiting for summer break to end."

Maisie laughed softly. "No kidding. They say the days are long, but the years are short. If that doesn't sum up parenthood, I don't know what does."

"We have another new firefighter in town," Maisie offered in between bites of food.

"There are always new firefighters in town," Tiffany chimed in.

"Well, now there are four hotshot crews. That's twenty-five to a crew, so it's one-hundred firefighters," Maisie replied with a shrug.

My eyes went wide as I stared at her. "Seriously?"

"That's a lot of men," Tiffany commented.

"It's not all men," Maisie corrected. "Susannah's on the town crew. Paisley is about to transition to the town crew and Phoebe used to be a firefighter."

"There's Harlow," someone else chimed in. "She's only in town part-time and doesn't do that anymore though."

"Firefighting sounds exciting," I said.

Tish let out a sigh. "Falling in love with a firefighter is kind of stressful."

Tiffany cast her a quick smile. "It is. But then, statistically speaking, driving a car is riskier."

Tish chuckled before taking a bite.

"Statistically speaking, being a backcountry pilot in Alaska is really risky," Holly said.

"Does Nate enjoy being a pilot?" I asked.

Holly's blond ponytail bounced with her nod. "He loves it, but I worry whenever he handles the longer flights. He promises me he will always be careful when the weather is bad. He will probably fly for the rest of his life unless I can persuade him to change careers. He's looking into investing in that ski lodge that's being planned."

"Oh, he should totally do that!" Madison enthused.

"With Fireweed Industries expanding here and planning to open up a full-service location with the restaurant and winery, they are going to have tons of potential new customers. The only other ski lodge nearby is over four hours away in Diamond Creek. I love that one, but it's a drive," Holly explained.

"I've never even gone downhill skiing," I said.

"Never?" Holly glanced over.

"Never had a chance, and it's pretty pricey to go."

"I can hook you up with some passes at the lodge in Diamond Creek," Holly replied. "I'm friends with one of the owners."

"I have to get through my bar exam and then maybe I'll have time to breathe," I said.

"Well, let me know anytime you'd like to go. We could even plan a weekend trip there," Holly offered.

Tish met my eyes. "You are going to kick that exam's ass."

I took a quick breath. "I hope so. I do better under pressure, so I've scheduled it in a few months. In the meantime, my face will be plastered in textbooks when I have time to study."

Holly's husband, Nate, stopped by the table to greet the group. As he was walking away, I felt a prickle on the back of my neck and instantly knew Hudson was nearby. I tried to convince myself I was crazy, but then I heard his voice. Nate stopped and grinned. "Hey, cuz!" He threw an arm around Hudson's shoulder and gave him a quick squeeze.

They continued walking. Just when I thought Hudson probably hadn't noticed me, he glanced over his shoulder, his eyes instantly locking with mine. My pulse catapulted forward at a breakneck pace. For a few seconds, it felt as if there was a flame racing between us with sparks scattering high in the air.

My breath felt shaky when he finally looked away. Once again, Hudson's words echoed in my thoughts. Four days had passed, so what did that mean? To me and to him.

Chapter Sixteen
STELLA

My body, or rather my hormones, knew exactly what I wanted. In a strange twist, my mind wasn't fighting it. Oh, I was a little worried. I didn't think Hudson was an asshole, but I did worry that I might get in over my head.

Hudson seemed like the perfect candidate to help me leave my virginity in the dust. He'd already given me one orgasm. Two would make it even better.

When I let myself into the quiet house that night, I wondered how long it would be before he got home. I needed to say something before I lost my nerve.

I didn't have to wait long. I was in the kitchen taking a swallow of water when I heard the front door open. My heart thundered along in my chest like hoofbeats pounding on the ground faster and faster. Seconds later, Hudson walked into the kitchen.

As soon as my eyes locked with his, heat rose inside, my skin prickling all over. I set the glass down, resting my hand on the edge of the counter. My fingers curled around it. I needed something to hold onto.

"I've thought about it," I said without preamble.

He took a few steps into the kitchen, stopping maybe five feet away from me.

"What's your answer?"

Chapter Seventeen
HUDSON

Fifteen minutes earlier

"G'night," I called to the guys.

There was a chorus of goodbyes as I turned to begin walking out of Wildlands. Parker fell into step beside me. "I'm headed out too," he said.

It was kind of strange how familiar his presence felt. Parker and I had spent only a short time together, but it had been condensed and unlike any other part of my life.

I was *really* glad he was doing well. As I stepped out into the parking area and the door swung shut behind us, the sounds from the restaurant became muted. The air was crisp and cold and the stars bright in the winter sky as our footsteps crunched on the frozen gravel.

I stopped at the back of my truck and glanced over. "It's really good to see you," I offered.

His smile was wry. "Same."

"I'll catch you around at the station. You've got my cell now," I added. "Anytime you want to meet for coffee, or whatever, just text me."

He clapped me on the shoulder before he continued walking. "Of course."

A few minutes later, as soon as I pointed my vehicle toward home, Stella commandeered my thoughts.

My body felt drawn tight, leashed need rampaging through me as I tried to contain it. Stella stood before me, her riot of blond curls pulled up in a ponytail. She was wearing a big sweater that fell below the curves of her hips over a pair of fleece leggings and fuzzy socks. There was nothing particularly sexy about what she was wearing. But this was Stella. Everything about her was sexy to me. I wanted to smooth my hands over her soft sweater, knowing that what lay behind was beyond tempting.

"What's your answer?" I asked.

"Huh?" An adorable little furrow formed between her brows.

It had been four days since our last encounter in the kitchen when I told her to take a few days to think about it. Ever since, I'd pondered what "a few" meant to her.

A pause stretched like elastic between us before snapping tight and drawing everything inside me to a shivering tension. "When I said I didn't want to be friendly strangers and asked if you wanted more," I explained over the echoing thud of my heartbeat.

Stella blinked and her fingers tightened around the edge of the counter. I heard her breath draw in swiftly before she replied, "Yes."

My breath came out in a rush of relief at her answer. Obviously, I would've respected if she thought this whole thing was flat-out crazy. It was, but I wanted her too fiercely to think clearly.

Just now, my hands clenched into fists. I wanted to dive into the fire burning between us. Yet, I thought this warranted a little more conversation.

I cleared my throat. "Ground rules. This stays between you and me. There's no sense in having it get messy as far as rumors. If you change your mind, at any point, all you have to do is say so. While this is happening, it's just you and me. Any more ground rules?"

Stella's teeth dented her bottom lip as she uncurled her hand from her glass on the counter and pushed it away. The claws of need sank more deeply, the sharpness keeping me on edge.

"I don't think so," she finally said. "Well, except birth control. You wear condoms."

"Of course," I said without hesitation.

"Anything else?" she prompted.

"Where are we sleeping?"

Her brows flew up in surprise. After a charged moment, she lifted her chin. "We sleep in our own beds."

I nodded. "Anything else?"

Her ponytail swung as she shook her head.

"Do we start tonight?"

Stella's hand dropped away from the counter, her fingers catching her sweater and sliding back and forth on the hem. The time between my question and her answer stretched as the tension ratcheted higher. The air around us felt heavy, reverberating with the force of a lit fuse.

"Yes," she finally said, her voice a little forceful.

I'd expected her to say we should wait. While I grappled with that, she jumped in again, her words coming out in a rush. "If you want to wait, that's totally fine. I just kind of wanted to get it over with and –"

"Wait." I stepped closer.

Stella stared up at me, her cheeks stained a deep rosy pink and her lips slightly parted. When she slid her tongue across them nervously, need pounded inside of me, the driving pace increasing to the point of pain.

"Okay," she said quickly. "We wait."

"That's not what I meant. I don't want to wait."

Taking another step, I stopped inches away. I could feel the heat emanating from her, along with a subtle sense of restlessness. I lifted a hand to brush a loose curl away from her cheek. Catching the end of it, I spun it around a finger as I drew it out. The silky curl bounced when I released it.

Her palm landed on my chest, close to my heart. My heart lunged at the soft touch. "You don't want to wait?" Her voice was breathy, the soft sound spinning like fire in my veins.

I couldn't even speak, but I managed to shake my head. "Not unless you do."

Stella shook her head, her curls swinging slightly.

"Does that mean you want to wait, or you don't want to wait?" A laugh rustled in my throat at the double negative.

"I don't want to wait." Her words were clear as she looked up at me, the boldness shimmering in her gaze nearly made my knees give out.

I meant to take control of this situation, to grab a hold of the moment and bend it to my need. My need was rampaging through me, but it was out of control.

Stella erased what little distance there was between us. I felt the soft give of her curves against me, the warmth of her as she leaned up. I dipped my head and our lips collided. It was like metal striking pavement, scattering the sparks high and bright.

My rational brain tried to fire off instructions, trying to point out I needed to go slow, I needed to make this amazing for Stella. But the roar of need was like a storm raging out of control inside. She was the eye of the storm, and all I could do was hold on.

She made this little whimpering sound in her throat as our tongues tangled. I groaned as I angled my head to the side and slid my hand into her curls. I couldn't get enough of her sweet taste, and her soft curves. I slid my arm around her waist, giving in to the urge to slide it down her back and over her luscious bottom.

Her hand slipped under my shirt and the feel of her palm exploring my chest before sliding around my waist was intoxicating. Her touch was bold and curious.

I wanted *everything* all at once. We finally broke apart to breathe. I stared down at her, searching her gaze, looking for hesitation.

"Are you sure about this?" I asked.

Chapter Eighteen
HUDSON

"Yes," Stella rasped.

My breath was shallow. The storm inside felt like lightning striking dry grass, lighting little fires that burned hot and fast through me.

Once again, I meant to take control. And yet, Stella ripped it right out of my hands as if tearing up slips of paper and dropping them into the fire burning between us. She stepped back, hooking her hand on the hem of her sweater and lifting it up over her head in a swoop. Before I could fully absorb the sight of her wearing a black lace bra with her pink nipples visible through the lace, her hands hooked on the waistband of her leggings, and she shimmied out of them swiftly. My eyes were drawn to the triangle of black silk at the apex of her thighs before trailing down. She was flushed pink all over. Her fluffy socks were a playful contrast.

I cleared my throat, dragging my gaze upward, just as she gestured toward me. "You're wearing too many clothes," she pointed out with a saucy lift of her chin. Her lips curled in a teasing smile, although there was a hint of hesitance flickering in her gaze.

I moved with alacrity, reaching behind my head to hook my hand on the back of my T-shirt to tug it off and toss it behind me.

Stella's eyes darkened as she held my gaze before stepping closer. Once again, just when I thought I was going to gain the upper hand, she dragged her hand boldly over the swell of my cock through the denim of my jeans. Her fingers nimbly undid the buttons before her hand dipped inside and curled around my length.

My breath hissed through my teeth. "Stella," I bit out.

"No need to say please," she said. She pushed me back and my hips bumped into the counter behind me. "Do you mind?" Her eyes lifted to mine as her hands curled around the waistband of my jeans.

All I could manage was a sharp shake of my head. She pushed my jeans down around my hips, just enough to free my cock. Her eyes held mine as she shimmied down. Her tongue darted out to slide across the tip of my cock where cum was already leaking out.

My breath came out with a ragged groan when her lips closed around my crown, sucking lightly before her palm gripped at the base and she drew me fully inside her mouth.

Whatever I expected tonight, it wasn't for Stella to nearly slay me with her naughty mouth. I clung to the counter behind me with one hand and had my fingers buried in her curls just to keep from collapsing on the floor as she teased me with her tongue. The subtle suction of her teasing mouth had me seeing stars. I could feel my release threatening, sizzling like lightning inside.

"Stella!" I choked out.

She drew back, releasing me with a little pop. When she looked up at me with her big brown eyes, her cheeks flushed, and her lips, plump and glistening from sucking on my cock, I nearly came right then and there. I was supposed to be the one in control here. I wasn't. At all. She could've ordered me to do anything in this moment.

Scrambling inside, I grabbed onto the frayed reins of my control. "I want—" I had to pause to suck in a breath of air, needing oxygen to clear the haze of need in my thoughts.

"Just because I'm a virgin in one way, doesn't mean in *every* way." Her voice was throaty and sultry. With her palm still curled around the base of my cock, she slid it up and down slowly. "I want to do this. Is that okay?"

"Fuck, yes," I bit out.

Her tongue swiped across her bottom lip before she teased around my crown again and sucked me into her warm mouth. That was all it took. The threads of my control snapped and my release spurted out, just as she drew back once more.

When Stella stood up, my need for her was still burgeoning, like a storm rolling in across the ocean, but the unexpected climax helped me regain some control inside.

She stepped away and rinsed her hands in the sink, rather practical in the middle of the moment. When she turned back and her eyes snagged with mine, I saw the uncertainty flickering there. I tugged my jeans up, just enough to walk without looking like a fool. I took a few steps to stop in front of her.

"Your bedroom or mine?" I asked.

Her skin was already flushed, but at my question, the pink deepened. Her lips parted slightly as she took a breath.

"I like my bed," she answered.

"Lead the way."

She reached for my hand and led me up her stairs in her fluffy socks. Following her, I was treated to the stunning sight of her lush bottom, barely covered in black silk, as she walked up the stairs, her hips swinging with every step.

Thank fuck I'd already had my release. By the

time we got to the top of those stairs, I was hard as a tire iron again and nearly desperate for her.

I needed to keep my wits. I couldn't just throw her on the bed and fuck her roughly. I would have to save that for another day. The second that passed through my mind, for a flicker, my cynical voice, the one that was so sure I would never want anything other than casual with anyone, tried to shout out that thinking like that was crazy. But I swatted it away like the annoyance it was.

Chapter Nineteen
HUDSON

I couldn't hold myself back once we rounded the top of her stairs and began moving toward her bedroom. Her apartment was laid out exactly like mine, so I knew where I was going. I reached for her hips and spun her around, pressing her against the wall and kissing her.

She felt *so* good. She kissed with a sweet boldness. I nudged my knee between her thighs, savoring the way she rocked her hips over it, letting out these little whimpers in her throat. She broke away, crying out.

My heart thudded in resounding beats against my rib cage. There was something about Stella. She was sexy as hell, beautiful, and cute, and everything I wanted. But there was also a vulnerability to her that slipped like slivers of air through the sealed windows around my heart. The protectiveness I felt for her ran deep as a river. I distantly told myself it was because she was a virgin. That had to be it.

"Hudson, hurry," she pressed, her voice breathy and raspy.

We stumbled down the hall, spinning against the wall with kisses and hands exploring each other. Seconds later, we were in her bedroom. I nudged the light switch with my elbow.

Stella didn't wait for me. She flung her bra off, her breasts bouncing free, and I nearly choked. Her nipples were dark, dusky pink and her breasts plump and tempting. She moved to the bed, bending over and shimmying out of her panties before she kicked them off.

Her gaze swung to me. "You're wearing too many clothes," she announced.

When she turned toward the bed, I was galvanized. Her voice was the crack of a whip. I shucked my jeans, barely remembering to fetch a condom out of my wallet in my back pocket. It wasn't that I got that much action, but I knew better than to be careless and unprepared.

Stella was crawling onto the bed and started to turn over when I said, "Stay right there, sweetheart."

I rolled the condom on and moved behind her, sliding a palm down her spine, savoring the way she shivered under my touch. I slid a palm over the soft curve of her bottom, delving between her thighs and into her folds. She was so very wet. Her channel clenched around me when I sank two fingers knuckle-deep inside of her.

Tempting though it was to take her this way, I wanted to see her face when I filled her. I helped her turn over. Because I knew my control was fragile, I moved with deliberation. I stretched out over her. She blinked as she looked up at me, her legs curling around my hips.

She was impatient. "Hurry."

"Stella, I don't want to rush this."

Somehow, she lifted her chin as she stared at me. There was a flash of stubbornness in her gaze. "Maybe I'm a virgin, but I'm not fragile. I just want to get this part over with." She rocked her hips in emphasis, and I could feel the slippery slide of her folds against me.

With every ounce of discipline and control I could find, I reached between us, positioning my cock at her entrance. I started to slide in slowly, but once again she ripped my control away and arched up. I felt the tightness as I pushed through abruptly.

Stella's body tensed incrementally. I held perfectly still through several echoing beats of my heart. Her chest was rising and falling with her rapid breathing. Resting on my elbows, I took the weight off one as I smoothed her hair away from her cheeks. "Stella," I whispered.

Her eyes opened, and I was lost in the layered

depths of her gaze. I could feel her beginning to relax, the tight clench of her easing. "Are you okay?"

She blinked before leaning up and closing the distance between us to press a lingering kiss to my lips. "Yes," she whispered.

As I stared into her eyes, it felt as if the beat of my heart deepened. Something shimmied to life in the air between us, something beyond lust, beyond the need for her on a physical level. I didn't even know what to do with the feeling.

I waited another beat before shifting slightly. Her hips rocked up to meet mine, and we settled into an easy rhythm. I wanted nothing more than for this feeling to never end.

Chapter Twenty
STELLA

Hudson's eyes held mine as we rocked together. I was still startled, almost in awe of myself tonight. I felt free with Hudson. I wasn't completely without experience, I had just never taken things all the way before because it was usually difficult for me to relax. I'd never felt the way I did with Hudson.

I wasn't sure what came over me when I'd wanted to strip away his control, but it had felt empowering and helped me forget my anxiety about being a virgin. The burn of him filling me had passed. I was relieved. I hadn't wanted it to be too painful and it hadn't been. There'd been a burning sensation, an intense sense of stretching, and the feel of him filling me completely.

I was already chasing my release with the slick fusion of where we were joined. I wanted more, I wanted the relief. Pressure was building inside, a sense of tightness spinning faster and faster. At the very core of me, pleasure spun outward like a pinwheel shooting sparks.

I found myself begging, something I never could've imagined doing with any man. I felt raw and vulnerable with him.

"Hudson..." I gasped between broken breaths. "Please... I need..."

Hudson shifted slightly. For a breath, I missed all of him pressed against me. He reached between us and just as he drew back and filled me once again, he teased his fingers over my swollen clit. The pressure burst, pleasure breaking through me in a crashing wave, so intense my mind blanked. I distantly heard my ragged cry, followed by his name. On the heels of one more deep nudge inside of me, I felt him shiver all over as he held still before shuddering against me and rolling swiftly to the side when his weight came down almost heavily over me.

I was still reverberating from my climax. I collapsed against him. He adjusted me, carefully withdrawing. I felt as if I'd washed onto the shore after a storm. The sky was clear and bright now, the winds dying and the pleasure swirling through me in lazy eddies.

Hudson's hand sifted through my curls before smoothing down my back in a slow pass and coming to rest just below the dip of my waist. He cleared his throat, asking, "How do you feel?"

I felt alive, almost brimming with energy. Still awash in pleasure, I shifted my weight, resting an elbow on his chest as I rose up slightly and settled my chin on the back of my palm. I could feel his heartbeat, strong and true. "Really good," I said, unable to keep myself from smiling.

His eyes twinkled and I loved the way they crinkled a little bit at the corners with his slow smile. Even now, after all of that with my body sated and relaxed, my belly swooped a little. *This* man. Sweet hell.

"I can say the same," he said.

I could've stayed there and smiled at him for hours, which was really kind of ridiculous.

"I don't want to get up," he eventually said. "But I need a quick bathroom break."

Rather than waiting for him, I got up and padded into the bathroom with him. He tossed his condom into the trash.

Hudson studied me, and I took a moment to just appreciate the man. He was all rugged muscle. Not in a polished way, but in a lived-in way. His shoulders were broad, his chest muscled. My eyes trailed down over his strong thighs. "How's your knee?" I asked.

"Good to go," he said with a chuckle. "Physical therapy worked wonders and they cleared me about a month ago."

He caught me by the hand and pulled me into the shower with him. He kissed me against the tiled wall. After that, we toweled off.

"I need to check on Butter," he said.

"The very cat responsible for that knee problem. How come I haven't met your cat" I asked.

Hudson chuckled and I could literally feel the sound of it reverberating along my nerve endings. "I had already dislocated it, but yeah, I've been keeping him downstairs since you moved in."

"Well, you don't have to do that. He can run free. He can even come up here."

Next thing I knew, he took me down to meet Butter. I burst out laughing when I saw the cat. He was a soft blond cat, basically butter-colored.

Hudson lifted him into his arms and nuzzled him. "You sure you don't mind him being all over the house?" he asked. I could hear the cat's purr from several feet away.

"I'm positive. We can put the litter box on the center floor and he can roam."

"Just so you know, the minute you leave the door open to the upstairs he's going to explore," Hudson warned.

"Let's carry him up there now."

He set the cat on the floor and Butter twined around my ankles, purring away when I stroked between his ears and under his chin.

"He's a very friendly cat," Hudson offered as we approached the stairs to my apartment.

When we'd walked down to Hudson's apartment, we had left the door open to mine. Butter instantly raced up the stairs. After a quick tour of him investigating the space, he leaped onto my bed and sat in the middle of it, looking at us expectantly.

Even though Hudson and I had agreed there was no sleeping together, we broke that ground rule that very night. I blamed it on Butter.

We had to snuggle with him. We weren't savages. We curled up under the covers while Butter purred contentedly. I meant to not fall asleep.

When I woke during the night, draped over Hudson with Butter purring at our feet, I felt my lips curling into a smile. A tiny corner of my mind was worried and my heart was a little anxious, but it felt good so I didn't let myself dwell.

Chapter Twenty-One
HUDSON

Four days later

When I got home from a busy day at work, a massive moose was standing beside the front steps. Unable to get him to move along with a honk of the horn, I resorted to tossing a few snowballs at him, which finally encouraged him to amble into the trees. Once the coast was clear, I hurried inside. Butter greeted me at the door.

I actively ignored the shaft of disappointment at Stella's absence. She'd texted that she had meetings in Anchorage for work and wouldn't be home until later tonight. We'd completely broken our rule not to sleep in the same bed. We broke it every night.

My need for her felt like a river breaking through

a dam. I couldn't hold it back. I felt like a reckless teenager with her. While the raw want for her was fierce, I felt as if I was tumbling into something else. But I couldn't have more, most definitely not with Stella. She was about to be a lawyer when she passed the bar. If she knew about the shenanigans in my youth, she'd be horrified and rightfully so. I had come to a resigned peace with my past, at least for myself. Yet, I still winced inside when I thought about it. Much as I wanted to lay the blame at my father's feet, I couldn't. He might've been the one who started me down that path, but I kept going because I couldn't keep my head out of my ass back then.

My phone vibrated with a text and I glanced down. It was Griffin asking me to meet him and some of the guys at Wildlands for food and drink.

Me: *I'll be there.*

I didn't need to linger. The place felt empty without Stella here. I let Butter back inside and gave him some fresh food before leaving. A short while later, I was seated at Wildlands with Griffin, Parker, Nate, Beck, and Leo.

"Hey, that's mine," Beck said, snatching the last halibut bite out of the basket, just as Nate reached for it.

Nate rolled his eyes. "Dude, we already ordered two more baskets."

Beck shrugged, unabashed. "I'm fucking starving. I'm also exhausted."

"Why so tired?" I asked.

"Max has a cold, which means he sleeps like hell. Maisie also has a cold. She'll try to drag herself out of bed even if she's half-dead, but I try to make sure she doesn't do that," Beck explained.

Griffin chuckled. "You're a good man."

Graham arrived, sitting down beside Parker and glancing toward Griffin. "Who's a good man?"

Griffin thumbed to his side. "Beck. He's exhausted because Maisie has a cold and he was on kid duty during the night."

"Totally get it. It is so much easier to have a kid when there's more than one parent. When you're sick, you can actually get a break," Graham replied.

"No shit," Beck said, nodding vigorously. "I cannot believe you raised Allie on your own until she was a teenager. The toddler phase is like being in a race that never ends."

Graham chuckled as he leaned forward for his glass of water. "When I look back, I still don't know how I did it. I was so fucking young."

Parker was watching quietly, his gaze curious. Beck caught Parker's expression and offered, "Graham got his girlfriend pregnant in high school. She was the homecoming queen. Turns out, she didn't really wanna have a baby." He studied Graham for a moment. "Graham is the best kind of guy. He did it on his own all the way until Allie made it to high school and then he fell in love. Allie's in college now, right?"

Graham finished a swallow of water. "She is, and I can't believe it." He glanced toward Parker. "Madison and I met a few years ago. We have a toddler now, and it's just different than doing it by myself. It also makes me feel fucking old. The only upside to having a baby when you're eighteen—" He rolled his eyes. "Living without sleep was easier then. Now, it about kills me. What about you?" he asked, glancing between us. "You're single, right?"

Parker nodded, and I hadn't even noticed I didn't reply until Beck leaned forward, his eyes on me. "Who are you seeing?"

My mind instantly offered up a mental replay of the feeling of Stella soft and warm underneath me and the sound of her crying out just before she climaxed. I kicked that train of thought away as hard as I could. "No one."

I'd never doubted, ever, staying single. And yet, one freaking night with Stella and there were little doubts creeping in. What the fuck?

"How many kids do you have?" Parker was asking Beck.

"Two. I love being a dad. You'll figure it out one day," he said with so much confidence I couldn't help but laugh.

"You think we should be having kids?" I teased.

Beck's ready grin stretched wider. "It's made me a better man." He shrugged, adding, "But I completely support people who don't want kids. It's not for everyone."

Parker rolled his eyes just as Graham chuckled. "It's not. Kids are more permanent than a face tattoo."

I almost choked on the swallow of water I'd just taken. "That's one way to put it. Kids have feelings, unlike face tattoos," I pointed out dryly.

A few other guys joined us and the conversation carried on. I was enjoying Willow Brook and the firefighters based out of the station here. Hotshot crews had a vibe if you will. The tone set here was one of mutual respect and support with none of that overblown masculinity kind of bullshit.

As evening rolled along, I started to wonder when Stella might get home. Considering that I had wholeheartedly set those ground rules, I was shocking myself. I rarely got involved. I was committed to keeping things superficial. Stella seemed to be on the same page.

We'd yet to speak of how we'd broken a primary ground rule the very first night. I was trying not to dwell on what that might signify. I shouldn't care about it, but I did. My heart wanted to believe we might have something special.

"What do you think of Willow Brook?" Parker asked from my side.

I rested an elbow on the table as I glanced his way. "I like it. A lot. What about you?"

He tapped his fingers on the table. "I like it too. I'm hoping to stay here long-term. My dad is, well, being my dad. He says he's in love again." Parker shook his head slightly. "You know how it goes."

"Oh, I do," I said with feeling. "Any updates on your sister?"

Parker shrugged, his fingertips drumming more rapidly on the table. "In the waiting game. I sent her mom a message through the DNA place and she replied. I gave her my info, so if my sister ever feels like reaching out, maybe we'll meet."

I could see the uncertainty in his gaze. That was something you tried to mask when you were in detention. You never wanted to get too hopeful. Parker and I had some pain in common. Our dads ran in the low-level trouble circles and we didn't have our mothers around. My mom died when I was little and his wasn't around. "Speaking of family, do you ever hear from your mom? Sorry to bring up a painful subject, but you used to talk about her," I added.

His smile didn't quite reach his eyes. "It's okay. One of the reasons I always trusted you is you weren't afraid to bring up the hard stuff, at least not with me. Never did hear from her. Sometimes I'm pissed at my dad, but then I remind myself that even if he didn't know how to make money legally, he was there for me in his own messy way."

I chuckled, shaking my head with him. "I've had similar thoughts about my dad. In the end, we're all flawed and stumbling along doing our best. In a way, I feel lucky that I fucked up young. It forced me to try something different."

Parker laughed with me at that. "True story. I'm really glad to see you, Hudson."

For a beat, tears stung my eyes. My first few weeks in detention were probably the loneliest in my life. I was scared to death and I was a skinny guy at the time, not sure how to protect myself if anyone targeted me. Parker showed up and we ended up bunking together. At the time, he was skinny as hell, but tall. He was scrappy and fierce. It wasn't that I needed someone to fight for me, but he was angrier than me back in those days. Nobody wanted to fuck with him, not after one or two attempts. He never hurt anyone, but he knew how to handle himself in a fight. He was smart, quick, and knew how to take people down. He'd also been a true friend to me.

It felt really good to find him again. "I'm really glad you're here. Feeling kind of lucky about that," I said. "Even though we lost touch, I always counted you as one of my best friends."

Parker's smile was slow. He curled his hand in a light fist and held it up for me to bump. "Same."

As I drove home a little while later, I wondered if I could be honest with Stella about my past. These days, it felt *maybe* possible. Before, I had just wanted to run from it. My dad had dragged his own criminal record behind him like the albatross it was. Even though we bounced around, they were all small towns. Skagway, Fireweed Harbor, Haines, and even Juneau felt small.

My thoughts swung to my cousin Nate. Nate was another bright spot for me. He'd always been good to me when we were kids. My dad would ship me off to visit his parents. and Nate was one of those easy, welcoming guys. He made you feel like you belonged. Aside from my job, coming to Willow Brook meant being near him again.

When I saw Stella's car when I got home, need burned like a flashfire inside. I forced myself to try to quell my anticipation. I had a whole list of reasons why I shouldn't be getting all worked up. Not over her. Not over any woman.

I wished I could give myself the same slack I gave others. My criminal record was solely from when I was a teenager, and it all started because of my dad. And yet, I couldn't help but wonder if I hadn't gotten caught if I would be like my dad now.

As if he knew I was wondering about him, my dashboard lit up with a call with *Dad* flashing on the screen. I sucked in a quick breath, letting it out in a gust before I answered. In spite of everything, I loved my dad. He was a scrappy guy, getting by however he could. My dad would move heaven and earth for me if I needed anything.

"Dad," I said, my lips curling in the usual wry smile he elicited.

"Hey! How ya doin'?"

"I'm doing good, Dad. You?"

"It's been a whole week since I talked to you," he said.

My dad called me every week. I figured he would until the day he died. I knew it would hurt when I didn't hear from him. "I've been expecting your call. What's up?"

"Not much. Trying to stay out of trouble, and I'm doing pretty well so far."

I chuckled. "I'm proud of you, Dad."

My eyes stung a little. After most of his adult life, as far as I knew, running one illegal thing after another to make money, my dad had started this resale business online. It was all on the up and up. The man loved collecting things, always had. When he realized maybe he could do something with all the shit he'd collected, he did. He met some woman who was actually decent. She helped him set up a website and it was working.

"Dad, I hope it keeps up for you. I love you no matter what you do."

"I know, I know. I love you too. I wish I'd met a girl like Martha sooner. She's good to me. Makes me want to stay out of trouble."

I knew as well as anyone how hard it was to walk a straight line once the path you'd been following was crooked. It was hard to break away. I'd had a good probation officer who pointed me toward a job program. I did my community service at the fire station. Each little step was a cascade into something better for my life.

"How are you doing?" my dad pressed.

"I'm good, Dad. I like Willow Brook."

"How's Nate?"

"Pretty good."

"Give him a hug for me. Fire season should be getting busy soon, right?"

"In another few months." I glanced around at the snow still blanketing the ground.

"Well, my latest life advice is for you to find a good partner," my dad said.

A laugh rustled in my throat. "Seriously, Dad? Are you giving me romance advice now?"

"Martha's been a life changer for me," he insisted.

"Dad, you've always had a good heart. I'm just glad you found someone who sees it."

He laughed softly. "All right now. I'll catch you next week, okay?"

"You got it. Love you, Dad."

"Love you, son."

After the call ended, I turned off the engine and sat in the quiet for a minute. I suppose if my dad could settle down and find love, maybe I could. But Stella was a lawyer. She would have all kinds of opinions about my youth. There was misspent youth, and then there was running drugs with your dad and spending months in juvenile detention.

I shook those thoughts away and climbed out of the truck, the cold air striking my cheeks as I jogged into the house. Disappointment struck me when the kitchen was dark and there was no sign of Stella. Seeing as we'd broken our rules already, I wanted to keep breaking them.

Yet, we hadn't talked about what was happening. Every encounter was by chance every night. Butter came walking out of the kitchen, meowing up at me. He crossed over to Stella's door, pacing in front of it with his tail twitching as he purred loudly.

I kicked off my shoes and hung up my jacket, walking into the kitchen instead of going down to my apartment. Butter lingered in front of Stella's door for another minute before he stopped and sat down, staring up at it. I glanced over at him before pointlessly opening the refrigerator. I walked out to the back deck to look outside. The moon was crescent-shaped, shimmering over the icy lake outside and the stars were bright, like shards of diamonds thrown up against the inky black.

As I turned to close the door, I heard Stella. "Hey, Butter," she said conversationally.

I walked across the kitchen toward the entryway where the door to her place was. When she saw me, her eyes widened and pink crested high on her cheeks.

"Hi!" she squeaked.

She leaned down to pet Butter who was twining around her ankles, purring like crazy. His purr was as loud as the cacophony of the rising storm inside of my body.

We studied each other as she straightened.

"What do you want?" I asked.

Chapter Twenty-Two
STELLA

I stared up at Hudson, trying to gather my thoughts. Hudson had this discombobulating effect on me. It was like a wild, unexpected gust of wind blowing through me, scattering my thoughts and sending flames of heat flickering high.

I'd been trying to tell myself I needed to create some distance, to be practical. Most importantly, to remember why it wasn't smart for me to get too involved with anyone.

I knew, all too well, just how susceptible I was to being like my mother. She wore her heart on her sleeve and thrust it out at any man who came by. She wanted stability. She wanted someone to love her and take care of her. Her neediness and desperation had been taken advantage of for years.

I craved stability, and I wanted a boring life—bills paid, a roof over my head, and never to have to move again. Most certainly not to feel vulnerable and needy and to feel the threatening rise of the tide of wishing someone would love me. I'd built walls, tall and high, around my heart. Somehow, those walls had been breached by the water of need rising higher and higher. It might spill over and the little girl who wanted love just might drown.

I cleared my throat. My intellect, that rational, logical part of my brain, tried to speak. That low, calm voice couldn't be heard over the nearly overwhelming cacophony of my hormones.

I reached for Hudson's hand just as Butter went dashing by, racing up the stairs into my apartment. *Butter.* This was all his fault.

Hudson's lips quirked, bemused by Butter. My belly did a little swoop and my hormones spun like pinwheels.

Hudson's palm was warm and dry as it curled around mine and his thumb stroked along the outer edge of my wrist. I could've melted right there on the spot. That tiny strip of skin felt as if it were on fire, like a match tossed in dry kindling.

"We're breaking the rules," he said as he took a step closer, his eyes never once breaking away from mine.

"I don't care," I whispered.

In that moment, I didn't. I wanted Hudson. I

wanted more of the pure escape he offered. More of the way I felt safe when I was with him. I wouldn't pretend it was just the sense of safety. It was the sizzling chemistry, the way my guard fell with him, the way I could forget all of my reserve, all of my worries, the way I could let go of the sheer exhaustion of trying to never need anyone.

Falling asleep wrapped in his strong embrace created a sense of protection and belonging I had truly never experienced. If I thought about it, it terrified me. It was *that* intoxicating.

His eyes darkened as he bent low, pausing with his lips a whisper away from mine. "Good, because I want you." I felt the shape of his last two words on my lips.

The next few moments felt like a dam broke inside of me, the water rushing through with such force it washed away any barriers left. Our kisses were a messy tangle of lips and tongues and our teeth clanking. At one point, we broke apart long enough to begin yanking at each other's clothes. We stumbled up the stairs, barely making it to the top.

My shirt was somewhere halfway down the stairs in a rumple with the rest of my clothes. I savored the surface of his palms on my skin as he blazed a fiery trail of kisses down the side of my neck. I cried out when he sucked a nipple into his mouth, the sensation arrowing to the core of me as my pussy clenched.

"Hudson…" I gasped.

He lifted his head. I could feel the length of him against my low belly.

"Yeah?" His voice was ragged.

"I need you."

We stumbled a little as he kissed me, one of his hands sliding down my back to cup my bottom and press against me. He spun us around to where we were against the waist-high wall encircling the stairs. He turned me to face it, saying, "Bend over."

I obeyed without an ounce of hesitation. His palm smoothed down my back, his touch dallying over my bottom before he hooked his fingers over my panties and yanked them down. His knee nudged between my knees, pushing them apart slightly. I was so wet I could feel the moisture on the inside of my thighs. He dragged his fingers through the wetness, and I whimpered, arching my back slightly. I needed him inside of me. *Now.*

"Hudson, please—"

He sank two fingers inside of me and I trembled, crying out when he withdrew his touch. I felt him blowing over my sex before he brought his mouth to me, his fingers filling me again and again.

He teased me with his tongue and fingers to a fierce, rushing climax. Trembling all over, I was barely able to stand as I clung to the edge of the wall. I heard the sound of the condom wrapper. Seconds later, I felt the press of his thick crown at my entrance, he filled me in one surge while I was still experiencing the echoes of my orgasm.

I clenched around him as he filled me deeply, savoring the intense stretch when he seated himself fully inside. One palm slid up my back, his fingers lacing into my curls as the other curled around my hip.

"Once more for me, sweetheart," he rasped.

I arched back as he began to fuck me slowly from behind. It felt so dirty, the way he used my hair to bring me back each time he filled me. Curling over me, he slipped his hand around my hips to tease over my sex. I shivered at the feel of his teeth grazing my neck.

"Now," he whispered as he nipped my earlobe.

My climax ricocheted through me, the pleasure so intense I was trembling, my hands flexing where they curled over the edge of the wall. He pumped slow and deep once more before he went taut and shuddered with my name on his lips.

I held still with Hudson curled around behind me, trying to catch my breath, trying to come back from the pleasure. Somehow, I managed to stay standing as he withdrew. We stumbled into my bedroom and he pulled me into the shower after he tossed his condom in the trashcan.

He carried me to bed, and we fell asleep together again with Butter curled up at our feet. I woke during the night, feeling safe and secure with one of his arms banded around my waist where I was curled against his side like a little barnacle. I told myself I wasn't falling for him, not yet. But even then, in the darkness in my sleepy thoughts, I knew I was lying to myself.

Chapter Twenty-Three
STELLA

"You've got this," Tiffany said, her tone far more confident than the way I felt inside.

I pushed my glasses up on my nose. "What if it's weird?"

She shrugged. "I think it's guaranteed to be weird at first. You have a half-brother who you didn't know existed. On the positive side, he reached out to you. He obviously wants to connect."

My cheeks puffed out when I released the breath I'd been holding. "Maybe we should've met somewhere else."

Tiffany reached across the table for my hand. She had suggested meeting for lunch at the Gallery Café. Aside from it being a public location, there was a gallery connected to the restaurant, so we could walk around if we wanted.

She squeezed my hand before releasing it. "You miss one hundred percent of the chances you don't take. I don't know who first said that, but it's completely true. Maybe you'll meet your brother and never talk to him again. Maybe it'll be awkward, but you'll get to know each other. I saw the message he sent your mom. It seemed pretty straightforward. It's not like he wants to connect because you have money or anything shady. You're a struggling law student trying to pass the bar exam."

I laughed softly at that. "Excellent point. I grew up poor and I'm still poor. I hope to not be poor eventually, but that's how it is now."

Tiffany's smile was warm. "He's a hotshot firefighter. He's not rolling in the dough, but he has great benefits."

I snorted. "Excellent point."

"While we're waiting, can I persuade you to adopt a cat?" she asked.

"Hudson's cat runs free in the duplex, so I need to check."

Tiffany clapped her hands together lightly. "Butter! Hudson got him from the rescue."

"Huh?"

"Wes's mom runs the local animal shelter. He helps out there. As a result, I help out too. I'm always trying to pawn animals off on anyone I know.

I'd like to add that having a pet is excellent for your mental health. If you get a dog, you walk a lot. What about a dog *and* a cat?" She smiled encouragingly.

I burst out laughing. "One at a time, Tiffany."

I was still laughing when I heard, "Stella?"

Glancing over my shoulder, I saw a man who matched the photograph he'd texted me, Parker Grayson. Tiffany told me she and Wes had already met Parker at the station since they were both hotshots. That helped convince me to do this.

Parker glanced toward her. "Good to see you, Tiffany."

I swallowed. This felt more nerve-racking than meeting someone for a date.

"Hey, Parker," she said warmly.

I practically jumped out of my chair and thrust a hand out. "Hi!"

Parker looked as nervous as I felt and that actually helped me relax a tiny bit.

I brushed my palms down the front of my jeans before sitting back down.

Tiffany gestured to the chair across from me. "Sit."

As I looked over at Parker, I realized he had my eyes. I'd seen pictures of my father, but he'd been gone since before I could remember him. I knew I had his eyes because my mom had told me. While Parker shared my brown eye color and honey blond hair, otherwise, we didn't look all that much alike.

Parker smiled over at Tiffany as he sat down. "I'm glad you're here."

"Yeah?" she prompted.

He ran a hand through his rumpled curls. "This is a first for me. Never met a sister I didn't know I had. It doesn't surprise me that my dad fathered more than one child, but it's still awkward. Chase explained to me how he met his other siblings."

Tiffany nodded along. "Yeah, we did DNA testing and found out Chase had a whole passel of siblings." Her gaze flicked to me. "You've met my brother, right?" At my nod, she continued. "It was awkward, and I'm pretty sure Chase was way more stressed out about it than me, but it was good." Tiffany looked between us expectantly.

I took a breath. "It's good to meet you. I'm really glad you reached out to my mom. I understand from her that you're a hotshot firefighter. There's a lot of those around here." My words felt stilted, but the anxiety was starting to fade.

Parker's grin was a little crooked, and I liked the warmth in his eyes. "There are definitely plenty of hotshots here."

A waiter came to take our orders. Even though my anxiety and the awkwardness remained, it started to ease as we talked. Tiffany smoothed things along a lot.

"Tell me about your mom," Parker said at one point.

"My mom is—" I paused as I considered how to describe my mom. "She's awesome, really. Heart on her sleeve, loves everyone, but money was always tight and her childhood wasn't easy. She tried to find any man to love her as much as she loved the whole world. She didn't have the greatest judgment about it. That's not to say that your dad was a bad guy, but she kinda had a knack for finding people who, well, I guess struggled like she did. I love her to pieces." I swallowed through the rush of emotion tightening in my chest. "What's your dad like?"

"Well, he's our dad," Parker said with a hesitant smile. "But he's—" He let out a sigh, the air reverberating through his lips as he shook his head. "He's a good guy who hasn't made the best choices in life. He means well, but he's always looking for the shortcuts. He also had a rough childhood and his parents scraped by doing sketchy things. That's pretty much what he's done as an adult. It's only been the last few years that he's stopped getting in trouble. It's probably for the best that your mom and him didn't stay together because he spent a lot of my childhood bouncing in and out of jail. Whenever he was in jail, I stayed with my aunt, who was also struggling, but not in jail." Parker's laugh was dry and a little sad. "I love my dad. He's always tried to be there for me. I hope you can love him too. He has no idea that I found you because I figured you might want to make that call yourself."

"Did he ever talk about me? My mom said he was in town when I was a toddler, but not really around. She said she knew I was his, but he was in trouble, so she steered clear. She didn't give me his last name or anything."

Parker shrugged. "From what I understood from your mom, he didn't know about me when he was in contact with your mom. My mom bolted when I was in kindergarten and left me with him. He became an instant dad." He paused, studying me for a beat. "We match," he said with a grin, gesturing to our matching blond hair.

Tiffany glanced between us, her smile kind. "I love this."

"If you want to let him know we found each other, that's fine with me. I'm not sure I'm ready to meet him, but it's okay if you tell him."

The waiter interrupted us to drop off the check, which Parker insisted on covering.

When we were walking out a few minutes later, he stopped and studied me. "By the way, I'll let my dad know, but I won't pass on your contact info until you tell me to. Is that okay?" At my nod, he continued, "What do you think about trying to get to know each other? I've never had a sibling. It was always just me, my dad, and my aunt. Any new family is great for me."

I didn't even hesitate. "I'd like that."

Chapter Twenty-Four
STELLA

I tilted my head to the side as I studied the picture on Tiffany's phone. "It looks like another Butter." She tapped the screen to zoom in. "I'm sure they'll love each other to pieces."

I laughed as I glanced over at Tiffany. "They might. Let me just ask Paisley. She's coming this way," I commented. Paisley was the friend who rented the apartment to me.

We were having a night out at Wildlands. So far, it was Tiffany, Tish, me, Paisley, Maisie, Phoebe, Alice, and Piper.

"Ask Paisley, what?" Paisley asked as she shrugged out of her jacket.

"About a cat. Tiffany is trying to convince me I should adopt a cat. I'm all for a cat, but I need to check with you because you're my landlord. I also need to make sure any cat gets along with Butter," I explained.

Paisley rolled her eyes. "Please don't call me a landlord. It sounds like I might be controlling."

"Um, the person who rents me a duplex? That seems like a lot of words," I pointed out.

Piper giggled from across the table where she sat beside Alice. "It does seem like a lot of words. You're a landlord. I'm a veterinarian, and I support this plan."

"Which plan?" Paisley prompted.

"The adopt-a-cat plan," Piper replied.

I snorted. "I support it too, but we have to make sure any new cat gets along with Butter."

"If they don't like each other, they'll sort it out," Alice offered.

"You can have another cat, pets are in the lease," Paisley added.

"Okay, can I come to meet the cat, and does she have a name?" I turned my attention to Tiffany again.

"Biscuit," Tiffany said.

"Was that on purpose?" I asked.

Tiffany shrugged. "I honestly don't know. They are the same color and so are biscuits and butter. Let me know when you can go meet her."

Alice waved at someone, saying, "It's the guys."

I could feel Hudson's presence before I even saw him. My skin tingled with awareness, and my pulse began to race. It felt as if my mind and my hormones were in a battle for dominance. For the most part, my mind won that war. My mind had learned its lesson. I knew the mistake of letting my hormones, much less my heart, take precedence. Even as a little girl, I promised myself I would never be as careless and desperate as my mother. Yet, in my young adult years, instead of getting wiser, I'd had a few years of stupid mistakes, thinking some guys had my best interests at heart when really all they wanted was a little fun.

It's a little benefit with Hudson. That's it, I told myself.

My hormones cheered, while my heart did a cartwheel, trying to show off. Meanwhile, Alice's husband Jonah was leaning down to give her a kiss and Tiffany was introducing me to Wes, saying, "I've convinced Stella to come meet Biscuit. I think they'll be a perfect match."

Wes chuckled. I managed to carry on something like a polite conversation while Hudson was talking with Nate.

"I think Biscuit is perfect because Hudson has Butter," Tiffany said, her smile satisfied.

Hudson glanced over, his brows hitching up in question. "What about Butter?"

"Tiffany wants me to adopt a cat named Biscuit. I told her we have to make sure Biscuit and Butter get along," I explained.

I glanced up toward Hudson, heat blazed through me. "What do you think?" I sounded breathless.

"Butter's pretty easygoing. I'm sure he'd like a friend," Hudson replied.

"I told Tiffany I could meet Biscuit tomorrow. Will that work?" I glanced up toward Wes.

I objectively noted he was seriously good looking with his shaggy dark blond hair and cognac eyes that crinkled at the corners with his grin. "Of course," he said easily, oblivious to my train of thought as I wondered why so many hotshot firefighters were handsome.

I had no reaction to any of them. Except Hudson. Anytime he was nearby, my pulse took off and anticipation buzzed through me. I felt like a foolish girl with a crush. I told myself it would pass. We were just having a little fun together.

Chapter Twenty-Five
STELLA

I gasped, my head falling back against the tiled wall as Hudson adjusted me in his arms.

"Stella," he rasped.

I dragged my eyes open, instantly ensnared in his dark gaze. My heart thudded with resounding certainty. He withdrew and thrust to fill me once again. A sense of intimacy shimmered in the air around us.

Moments later, I was still trembling all over. I walked on wobbly knees out of the bathroom and collapsed on the foot of the bed. Every single night, I told myself we couldn't do this every night. And yet, all of my internal promises were pointless. My body craved Hudson, while my heart was starting to get too involved.

He came out of the bathroom with a towel around his waist. My eyes tracked him as he walked over to me. The man was ridiculously built. He was all muscle with broad shoulders, his arms rangy and lean, and his chest tapering down to delineated abs. Even on the heels of an intense encounter with him and an earth-shattering orgasm, my awareness perked up a little at the sight of him.

He stopped a few feet away. We'd stopped even discussing where we should sleep. As if in punctuation, Butter jumped on the bed curling up beside my hip and purring loudly.

"I think we should bring Biscuit home." Hudson's eyes flicked down to Butter with a bemused smile.

"You do?" I asked.

"Bring her home. We'll see how they get along."

I was trying to get my mind on track. My thoughts were sluggish, practically melted from the heat of our encounter. "I can't imagine we'd take her back to the shelter."

His slow smile sent my belly into a tumble. "Probably not."

A few minutes later, I was curled up against Hudson's side in bed. "Tiffany says Biscuit is really sweet."

Hudson smoothed a hand over my hair and down my back in a slow pass. My heart kept on thumping, strong and certain. Once again, I tried to ignore the voice calling out that maybe this time was different. I couldn't ever let myself want someone like that.

Chapter Twenty-Six
STELLA

I laced my fingers together under the table, trying to contain the tension humming inside.

Parker smiled at me. "Are you okay?" he asked politely.

I let out a low laugh. "I am. This is kind of strange, you know?"

He cocked his head to the side. "Oh, I know. I'm just glad we connected."

For a few minutes, our conversation was stilted again. I figured it might be like this for a while. After we got through the initial awkwardness, it was easy. I liked Parker. Beyond being a nice guy with an understated sense of humor, I sensed he was a man trying to do better in life. When he spoke about our father, I could feel the underlying love and an almost resigned acceptance of what sounded like a chaotic, unstable childhood.

After we talked for a while, he leaned forward, resting his elbows on the table. His gaze became serious.

"What is it?" I prompted.

His shoulders rose as he took a deep breath. "I promised myself I was going to be honest with you."

"Okaaaay," I said slowly. "I promise I don't bite."

"I know." His lips twisted to the side and he eyed me cautiously. "You're finishing law school and studying for the bar, so I figure maybe law is important to you. I didn't make the best decisions when I was younger."

"Who does?" I countered. "Plenty of us do dumb things, especially when we're younger." My specialty was falling for assholes, but I left that out for now.

He nodded soberly. "As you know, my dad bounced in and out of jail. When I was in high school, he dragged me into it. I want to say it's all his fault, but at first, it seemed exciting to me. I felt cool and tough. Not that dealing drugs is cool, but you get my drift. I spent six months in juvenile detention as a result."

He went quiet at that, and the sound of him swallowing was audible. He held my gaze, and I could see the anxiety flickering in his eyes. He was bracing himself for me to judge him harshly.

"Are you expecting me to run away from the

table now and pretend like we never met?" I finally asked. I shook my head sharply. "We share the same father. Maybe my mom didn't get caught up in illegal things, but your dad isn't the only one—" I paused, considering how to phrase this. "With questionable life choices. It sounds like you've tried really hard not to let that follow you into adulthood, and I really respect that."

Parker's shoulders sagged and his head dipped down toward the table. He tunneled his hands through his hair as he straightened and let them fall flat to the table. "Thank God. Some people still think getting in trouble in high school marks you forever."

I rolled my eyes. "Look, I did go to law school, but my initial interest in it was because I wanted to make sure I made enough money that I didn't end up living life like my mom. I love her so much, but she's always been looking for someone to take care of her because she barely gets by. She dropped out of high school. She eventually got her GED, but it's been hard for her to find steady work. I wanted some stability." I took a breath, gathering courage. "She's been in a few abusive relationships. She assures me our dad wasn't abusive."

"Dad's never been abusive," Parker cut in.

"I'm glad to hear that. And back to your worries, I'm not all judgy just because I want to be a lawyer. I promise," I added.

He smiled a little. "Maybe you don't need to know this, but I haven't been on anything other than the right side of the law since the trouble I got into in high school. One of the best friends I ever met was when I was in detention."

I held his gaze, feeling my lips slowly curl into a smile. "That's good. Life is never simple and I'm glad you're doing better now."

He took another deep breath in and let it out in a whoosh. "Well, that's good."

"What's good?"

"That you don't think I'm a loser."

"Parker! Of course, I wouldn't think that," I protested.

He shrugged. "Some people do."

I studied him for a few beats. "Did you think you'd tell me this and I'd pretend like I don't want to be your sister?"

"I didn't know." His gaze was earnest and serious. "Once I knew you existed, I promised myself I'd let you know the truth from the beginning so you didn't think I was hiding it."

My chest felt tight, and I breathed slowly through it. "I'm really glad you reached out."

His smile was slow. "I can be your big brother now."

I rolled my eyes. "I'm pretty used to handling things myself."

"I mean, if you need me to kick somebody's ass, or threaten to," he corrected quickly.

I burst out laughing at that. "I guess I appreciate that."

"I haven't even told my dad I found you yet."

"My mom told him. She kind of can't help herself. She's all excited about us being a family now," I said dryly.

"It seems like they're both in better places than they were when they were younger. It's a goddamn miracle my dad isn't up to his old shenanigans and is actually making a living legally."

Parker's voice held a hint of disbelief, and I couldn't help but laugh again. "Although my mom hasn't lived a life of crime, she squeaked by. She sounded pretty happy to hear your dad's doing better. She says they want to come visit us."

"How do you want to handle that?" he asked.

I leaned forward as I waggled my brows. "We'll deal with it when it comes. Meanwhile, let's try to grab coffee at least every other week or so. My schedule's a little crazy these days because I'm studying for the bar, but I want us to, well, be siblings."

Parker's eyes were bright as he smiled. There was an earnestness to him that I liked.

A few minutes later, we walked out and, impulsively, I gave him a hug. It just felt right. "I'll see you soon," I said when we stepped apart.

"Absolutely," he said.

When I drove away a few minutes later, all the anxiety I'd been feeling around this had dissipated. I felt surprisingly good. Parker was a genuinely nice guy. I contemplated calling my mom, but I wasn't ready for her to freak out over my feelings on this because that's what she would do. I decided to give it a few days before I updated her. It felt serendipitous that Parker ended up in Willow Brook.

———

A few weeks passed, and Parker and I settled into a comfortable pattern. We got together for lunch or coffee about once a week. I finally told my mom that we'd met and I felt good about it. She was excitedly planning a trip with our dad. I didn't even know what to think about their rekindled romance. She declared it to be "fate" and was thrilled.

Chapter Twenty-Seven
STELLA

Aside from everything else happening in my life, there was Hudson. I was trying to keep him in a compartment in my mind and heart, but it was a challenge.

Every night, I went home. *To Hudson.* I was tumbling deeper and deeper into the heat of our connection. I tried to convince myself it was just chemistry. Every time, my heart chirped up and pointed out the obvious. *You're falling in love with him.*

For reasons I didn't completely understand, we didn't talk to each other much beyond the superficial. And yet, I found myself wanting to confide in him, to tell him about Parker. Realistically speaking, he likely knew Parker. They were both firefighters. That made me more reticent about it. It felt as if I could keep my personal details at a distance, then I wouldn't fall in love.

That alone should've prepared me for just how messy things could get.

Chapter Twenty-Eight
HUDSON

While I was valiantly trying to keep my emotions at bay, I knew I was treading in risky waters. Every single night, my need for Stella pounded like a drum in my body, the crescendo getting louder and louder by the night. I couldn't wait to get home. *To Stella*.

And yet, I knew it was a problem. I thought about her whenever there was a spare moment. The idea of not falling asleep with her curled up against my side, or me spooning her from behind, was something I didn't even like thinking about.

Spring was coming. Soon, I would be gone for weeks at a time. I would miss her. I'd never been in love, so I had nothing by which to measure my feelings for her. If I wasn't already in love with her, I knew I was well on the way. I wondered if the fall included a rock bottom where my heart cracked into a million pieces.

I didn't know if it was conscious on her part, or mine, but we were both keeping conversations to the surface. We talked about our lives superficially. I didn't tell her about my past and I was still anxious about it. I feared her judgment and what it might mean for us.

In the small town of Willow Brook, our social circles overlapped, but our encounters were passing in town. We had yet to be open about what was happening.

If any of our mutual friends suspected anything, there was only one person who commented on it. One morning, I was at Firehouse Café getting two trays of coffee for the station.

Janet smiled over at me when I handed her a slip of paper with a list of drinks. Her eyes twinkled. "Good thing you got here during a quiet time."

"We have a meeting, so lots of coffee is needed," I explained.

"Understood." She began prepping the coffees. "Would you like some donuts?" she asked.

"Donuts? Is this a new thing?" I waggled my brows.

Janet tapped a button on the espresso machine. "Sure is. A woman who moved to town is starting a bakery. She's using the space next door for now. It's gonna be a bit before it's up and running, so I told her she could do some baking here. She made a bunch this morning. They are delicious, I promise."

"Give us two boxes. You know how many firefighters there are," I said dryly. "They'll be gone within the hour, if not sooner."

I paid with the wad of cash the guys had thrust at me on my way out of the station.

"Tell me something," Janet said while she continued getting drinks ready.

"What's that?"

"What's up with you and Stella?"

If I thought I could play it cool, Janet caught me off guard. "What?" I sputtered, my eyes going wide.

Her grin was sly. "I knew something was up."

"Janet," I warned.

"I like Stella, and I like you."

I laughed softly as I shook my head. "Of course you noticed something. Look, it's not public knowledge and—" I let out a breath. "I don't really know what to say the status is with us because, well, because I don't know."

Janet studied me while she tucked the various coffees into one of the trays. "What's your story?"

"Uh, what do you mean?"

"Everybody has a story about why they don't want to fall in love, or why they want to avoid complications. I might be old, but I understand the heart pretty well. When I was young, I was an idiot."

"I don't even know how old you are," I pointed out.

"It's more than six and a half decades. Anyway, my parents had a shitty marriage."

"Oh, I'm sorry," I began.

She waved dismissively. "It wasn't like they beat me or each other, but they didn't like each other. They weren't of the generation to get divorced, but I wish they had. I was kind of stupid when I was younger. I was always looking for someone who wanted to commit too soon. After I broke my own heart a few times, I got lucky and I met my husband. He was a good man. It took us a little bit to figure things out because I was a little cynical by then. I still miss him." Her eyes were bright with tears.

"What happened?" I asked softly.

I knew Janet's husband had passed away, but I didn't know what had happened.

"He was one of those ice road truckers, you know how they have the reality show now?" At my nod, she continued, "He died in an accident one winter. I miss him, but I'll always be grateful for the time we had."

"I'm sorry," I offered, feeling as if that was completely inadequate.

"Thank you," she said softly. She was quiet for a moment as she finished getting another drink ready and slid the second tray over to me. Her gaze was perceptive as she held mine. "Maybe I don't know all the details and you don't have to tell me, but I'll say this, no matter what your story is, if it feels right with someone, it's worth the risk."

I swallowed and took an unsteady breath. "You think?"

"I know it is," she said firmly.

I ended up telling Janet my story, including my beyond-stupid choices in high school. I didn't tell her the whole truth though. I left out that I was afraid I didn't have it in me to be a partner to someone. I'd never witnessed a healthy relationship, so it felt foreign to me.

But maybe Janet was right, maybe it could be different for me.

Chapter Twenty-Nine

HUDSON

Later that day, I was hanging out with Parker after a workout. Because he was that kind of friend, I found myself thinking maybe I should ask his opinion.

"I'm curious about something," I began.

"What's that?"

"Do you ever imagine yourself getting serious with someone?"

"Well, if Beck has his way, I'll fall in love and get married because marriage is the best thing ever," Parker offered dryly.

I snorted. "True story. But, I'm serious. I've always kind of thought it wasn't for me because my past is a little messy and I don't have a single role model for a good relationship."

Parker studied me. "I get it. We're kind of in the same boat there. I don't know. I know you're a good man and a really good friend. You could also be a good boyfriend or husband, I guess."

He fell quiet, but I sensed he wanted to say something else, so I prompted, "What is it?"

"My sister."

"What about her?"

"We met. I haven't talked about it because it's pretty fresh. It's kind of crazy because her mom and our dad reconnected. They got back together. If you can believe it." He rolled his eyes. "They're all happy about it. I like my sister. I think we could actually be decent siblings."

"Wow." I nodded slowly. "I'm happy for you. Where is she?"

"Turns out she lives here. She moved here a couple of months ago, a little bit before me."

"You're fucking kidding me."

Parker shook his head. "Nope. She's here."

"I'm really happy for you."

"Enough about me, tell me who you're falling in love with," Parker said bluntly with an exaggerated brow waggle.

It felt as if he kicked my heart over. "What the hell do you mean?"

"Maybe it's been a minute since we hung out, but I know you pretty well. You're asking me because you're worried about your feelings for someone."

I stared at him and let out a sigh. "I didn't expect her. She, uh—" I cleared my throat. "So the place I live, it's kind of a duplex. There's a shared space between the two apartments. She lives in the upstairs apartment. Her name is Stella."

Parker was lounging on the couch, completely relaxed. As soon as I said Stella's name, he sat up abruptly, his feet landing flat on the floor. "Stella?"

"Yeah, what's wrong?"

"Last name Lancaster?" he pressed.

"Yeah?"

Parker closed his eyes, leaning his head back before he leveled his gaze with mine again. "That's my sister."

"No way." I shook my head, as if that would change the situation.

"Paralegal, just finished law school, studying for the bar, works for Blackthorne Law here in town," he recited the details about Stella.

"Oh, my God," I said slowly.

Parker narrowed his eyes. "You'd better not hurt her."

I held both hands up in surrender. "Dude, I'm talking to you about her because I'm pretty sure I'm in love with her."

I was scrambling inside. I was terrified to be in love with anyone. And yet, I was falling in love with Stella and my heart had zero doubts.

"Fuck!" Parker ran his fingers through his hair as he stared back at me. "Does Stella know?"

"Does Stella know what?"

"That you're in love with her. Have you told her your whole story?" he demanded.

I dropped my head forward into my hands, feeling my ragged sigh filter through my fingers. When I lifted my head again, I didn't even have to say anything.

Parker knew the answer. "You'd better tell her."

"I will. Look, I didn't plan this. Stella told me she didn't want to get serious. I'll tell her, but that's probably the end of it. She's gonna fucking hate me."

My friend shook his head. "She knows my story."

I drew in a slow breath, steeling myself mentally as I nodded. "I'll talk to her."

―――

When I arrived home and saw Stella's car there, my anticipation for her kept humming along inside. But now, it was mingled with a subtle anxiety and almost dread. I wasn't ashamed of my past. A lot of feelings about the trouble I had gotten into were linked to my father. I knew perfectly well that he had struggled to straighten his life up in part due to how many people judged him for his mistakes. I was deeply proud of him now. By no means was his life perfect, but he'd made some actual changes. He was trying to do the right thing.

I wasn't sure how to address this with Stella. In my heart, I knew most of my anxiety around this was because I was in love with her. It was one thing to break our rule about not sleeping in the same bed, but it was something else altogether to fall in love with her. I could run straight toward a fire in the wilderness, but the idea of bearing my heart was terrifying, and I wanted to run away from it.

When I walked into the kitchen a few minutes later, taking longer than I usually would to shrug out of my jacket and put my boots in the tray by the door, Stella was rinsing a glass in the sink. Her blond curls were pulled up in a messy ponytail. I wanted to walk up behind her and smooth my hands down her sides and nuzzle her neck. I loved how she always smelled a little sweet.

"Hey," I said. Even I noticed that my voice sounded strange, almost stilted.

She set the glass in the rack beside the sink and dried her hands on a dish towel. Her lips curled in a smile and my heart tripped and stumbled. Fuck me. This woman, so sweet and independent. She was everything I'd never expected and so much more.

Stella read the room instantly. "Is everything okay?" Her eyes searched my face.

It didn't surprise me, not even a little, that she knew something was weighing on me. I let my breath out in an abrupt gust. "You know how I mentioned I had a good friend who moved here?"

Her brows rose up. "Uh-huh."

"Well, it turns out he's your brother, or I guess your half-brother."

"Parker?" Her voice squeaked on the second syllable.

"Yeah."

Her eyes went wide as she lowered her hands, absently tossing the dish towel onto the counter. "What... how... did this...?" Her questions kept starting and stopping.

I pressed my tongue in my cheek as I cocked my head to the side, letting out a wondering chuckle. What I said next shocked me.

"Parker was one of my closest friends in high school. We met in detention. I was afraid to tell you because I thought you might judge me, what with you being in law school and everything." I made the sign of the cross in front of my chest. "I'm not the most religious guy, but you need to know I'm not lying. I haven't gotten in any trouble since then. I promise. Just like Parker, I had a dad who didn't make the best decisions and I got pulled into it. It's not my dad's fault, but it didn't help."

My words came out rapidly, each one sharp. I felt as if I was punctuating all my old feelings as I spoke. When I finished, I felt a sense of huge relief. Maybe my heart would crack if I lost Stella over this, but it wasn't as if I'd ever had her to begin with.

She was completely silent. I didn't know how long it was before she spoke, but each second felt like forever. She slowly tipped her head to the side, her eyes warm. "I wouldn't hold that against someone."

It felt as if my heart clapped, the sound loud inside my head. My shoulders sagged as I let out a deep breath. I rested a hand on the counter beside me as I dipped my head and sucked in another gulp of air. "Well, that's a relief," I said when I lifted my head.

Her lips teased a little at the corners. "I hope you wouldn't think I was that harsh and judgmental."

"If my past belonged to anyone other than me, I wouldn't think you would be. I don't exactly think clearly about my own mistakes."

Her chin dipped in acknowledgment. "I understand that." After a beat, uncertainty darted through her eyes. "We don't talk much about ourselves with each other."

"No, we don't," I agreed.

As our eyes connected across the distance between us, it felt as if something shimmied to life. I had become accustomed to the feeling of intimacy I experienced when we were together. That feeling was connected to our fiery hot encounters and the aftermath of being twined together.

This, here and now, was linked to that intimacy, but it ran deeper. The acknowledgment of how we tried to keep things to the surface made it so very obvious that something else had flourished, something beyond our control.

My heart thumped several rounding kicks in my chest, my ribs reverberating from the force.

Stella cleared her throat. "I understand more than you could imagine about having a parent whose life is messy. As you probably know from Parker, I don't remember my dad because he wasn't around. What I knew about him was that he was in and out of jail a lot. That wasn't the kind of chaos I had in my life, but my mom—" Stella's eyes contained a sense of resignation and love. "I love my mom. So much. But she never had good judgment about men and my dad was just one of a long string of not great guys. I originally wanted to go to law school for the money. I desperately didn't want to be scraping by and relying on a man, or anyone else, to bail me out. After I started law school, I realized it mattered because I could maybe help people. Something like that." Her lips twisted to the side with a self-deprecating smile. "All of that to say, I understand. When your childhood is a little bumpy, you eventually figure out that you just don't know anyone's whole story."

"No, you don't," I said slowly. Hope was unfurling inside of me. And yet, I wasn't ready to face what my heart was hoping for.

She cleared her throat again. "I'm not used to

having an older brother. How did this even come up with Parker?"

"Honestly, this –" I paused, unsure of how to put my thoughts and feelings into words. "Thing between us—" I gestured back and forth. *What the hell? You're calling it a thing.* I ignored my asshole of a mental critic and forged on. "I started to talk to Parker about it. He connected the dots and realized it was you."

"What is this *thing*?" she pressed.

We stared at each other. All the while the air felt as if it was filled with a shower of sparks—emotions, intimacy, and the fierce desire that bound us together—all flickering around us. "I don't know. Uh, and we haven't even talked about whether we're telling anyone about us. If I'd any clue who Parker was to you, I wouldn't have said anything."

Stella shrugged. "It's okay. He is my brother, but he's new to me. Was he all awkward about it?"

I let out a dry chuckle. "He warned me not to hurt you."

Her eyes widened slightly. "Are you serious?" Her tone was disbelieving.

"Yup, that's what he said."

Her cheeks flushed pink and she let out a wondering laugh. "Well, that seems a little ridiculous."

"If I had a little sister, I would feel protective," I offered.

While this whole thing had come about because I didn't know what to do with the feelings that were burgeoning by the second inside of me, I felt a little defensive that Parker would feel the need to warn me. I had no fucking clue how to do a serious relationship. I'd certainly never hurt Stella knowingly, but what if I couldn't be the man she needed? What if it didn't even matter? What if she didn't feel the way I did?

After a long moment, she shrugged again. "I'll talk to him. I don't need an overprotective older brother. Nobody, much less my brand new to me brother, has any say in my love life."

At the word "love", I wanted to grab it out of the air and hold it close, to tuck it inside my heart.

"I guess I should ask if we are trying to keep this a secret. Janet suspects something," I said.

Stella's laugh sputtered out. "Of course she does. I love Janet, but she notices everything."

I turned to look out the window. With it being deep into winter, it was already almost fully dark. The moon was high in the sky with the stars bright in the darkness.

When I brought my gaze back to hers, uncertainty was flickering in her eyes. She curled her hand around the hem of her shirt and rubbed it between her fingers nervously.

I wanted to step close and wrap her in my arms. I didn't need to know why she was nervous, I simply wanted to make that feeling dissipate for her, to will it away.

Maybe she had only given me a slice of her story in this moment, but it felt as if she'd opened a door into her heart, into understanding her in a way I hadn't before.

While I couldn't fully grasp it this moment, the enormity of what had happened for me wasn't lost. When it came to relationships, I kept things on the surface. Always. Until now.

Stella's hand dropped away from the hem of her shirt as she lifted her chin. "We don't have to keep this a secret. But what are we doing?" She closed her eyes, letting out a soft laugh. "We set ground rules, and now I don't know what to think."

My lips twisted to the side with a wry smile. "We broke one of those rules on the very first night," I pointed out.

Her lips pressed together before another laugh filtered out. "We did. What is this?" she whispered.

My emotions felt visceral. This feeling between us was gathering force, like the air before a storm. I thought of winter in Alaska and the way you could smell snow coming before it fell. The more potent the storm, the stronger that subtle scent was in the air. It was difficult to describe to someone who'd never experienced it. This feeling was like that for me.

If someone had tried to describe intimacy before

I felt it, I wouldn't have understood. It wasn't words. Words went with it, just as actions went with it, but it was the feeling itself that shaped everything.

When it flickered to life between us, it felt as if cords were binding us, stitching us, tighter and tighter together. I took a slow breath as I tried to collect my thoughts into something sensible. What I eventually said felt inadequate.

"I don't really know. I don't want this to stop."

We stepped toward each other at the same time, two forces striking metal and sparks leaping into the air. I was lost in her eyes. Her lips parted as she looked up at me, her hand falling to my chest. Her touch was warm. My heart kicked forward against it.

The moment stretched between us, burning hot, until I cupped her cheek and bent to claim her mouth.

Chapter Thirty
STELLA

When Hudson's lips met mine and his fingers tangled in my hair, I felt an overwhelming sense of relief. Losing myself in him was the only way to slake my need.

My rational mind, my protective mind, was lost in the roar of the storm. I knew I was breaking all of my own rules, but I felt safe with Hudson. It was remarkable how intoxicating it was to feel safe.

Our kiss got messy fast, a tangle of lips and tongue, before we broke apart. We gulped in air, desperate for oxygen. We yanked at each other's clothes.

With my sweater in a rumple on the floor and my jeans kicked to the side, I got naked first, maybe because I was more impatient, or Hudson was more helpful. His chest was bare with his jeans hanging open as he lifted me onto the counter. My leg curled around his hips, and I watched through heavy-lidded eyes as he dragged his thick crown through my slippery wet folds.

"Fuck me," he muttered gruffly.

"Please do," I gasped when he stepped back.

"I need a condom," he bit out. He started to turn away, but I caught his hand.

"I'm on the pill." I took a shaky breath as we stared at each other.

Hudson's gaze burned into mine. "Are you sure?"

In the loaded space between us, I whispered, "I am."

He stepped closer again, one hand sliding around me to press at the base of my spine as he pulled my hips a little closer to the edge of the counter. He stepped between my knees, his eyes locked to mine. Even though this wasn't the first time for us, I felt the depth of our intimacy, the power of our connection. Tonight, in this moment, it felt very real.

Up to now, I'd been shying away from it, trying to ignore what my heart already knew. I wasn't quite ready to say it, but I knew I was falling in love with Hudson and there was no turning back.

It was like falling over a waterfall, the rush of it carrying me down. I could only hope that he would hold on tight and keep me safe.

"Stella," he rasped.

I looked into his eyes, ensnared in the heat of his

gaze as he notched his cock at my entrance and filled me in one slow thrust. "Stay with me," he ordered. His words were commanding, but soft. I didn't want to look away.

He fucked me slowly on the counter with deep thrusts, seating himself more deeply each time. With the way my legs dangled down, it created an intense friction where we were joined. Each time he filled me, the sensation was intoxicating. I was delirious from the pleasure of it, from the look in his eyes, from the intimacy shimmering around us like cinders falling from the sky.

My release began to build, drawing tighter and tighter inside. Little pings of pleasure reverberated outward in ripples through my body. He rocked inside once more, whispering, "Come for me, sweetheart."

I cried his name as the ripples rose to a crescendo inside. I heard my breath, ragged and broken. He drew back and thrust forward one more time. My name on his lips sounded almost like a prayer as he shuddered, and I could feel the heat of his release filling me.

His head dipped into the curve of my neck as he held me close and we trembled together.

Chapter Thirty-One
STELLA

After we untangled ourselves, Hudson carried me upstairs to bed. Butter curled up at our feet. While listening to the rumble of his purr, my heart felt soft and vulnerable. I was deep into the danger zone with Hudson. And yet, I didn't want to worry about it. Not now.

I was curled up against his side, tracing my fingers through the light dusting of hair on his chest. "I need to go meet Biscuit."

Hudson rolled his head to the side, opening his eyes. While the room was dark, there was a little light from the moon outside the windows.

"Biscuit?" he prompted, looking confused.

"The rescue cat that Tiffany's trying to get me to adopt," I reminded him.

"Oh, that's right." His lips curled into a drowsy smile. "If you like her, just bring her home."

As I drifted into sleep a few minutes later, my mind kept bouncing that word around—home.

Was home this place, or us?

———

The following morning, I tried not to get too caught up in the view of a naked Hudson as he toweled off after our shower. I tried not to think about the fact he'd just fucked me against the tiled wall in that shower.

This was all getting *way* too comfortable. My eyes lingered on the subtle flexion of his back muscles as he moved. I never knew I had a thing for backs. Maybe it was him. He was all lean muscle, his shoulders, his forearms, even his hands.

He turned toward me again and I almost groaned at the sight of his chest. Blessedly, he reached for a T-shirt. A moment later, he had on a pair of jeans and he was even putting on socks. This was all helpful for my ability to focus.

I already had on a pair of jeans and reached for my bra. I felt him standing in front of me as I reached to hook the clasp together between my breasts. He let out a low growl before he said, "Give me just a minute."

Before I could ask why, he cupped my bare

breasts, teasing his thumbs over them. When I glanced up and saw the heat banked in his eyes, my nipples tightened, my belly felt tickly from the butterflies, and the core of me clenched tight.

"Hudson," I whispered, feeling a flush rise to my skin.

"Stella," he murmured, his voice teasing when he bent low and sucked one of my nipples into his mouth before releasing it and blowing softly over it.

In a matter of seconds, I was slick and needy for him.

"I have to go to work," I choked out.

He stepped back, the sound of his low chuckle sending goosebumps chasing over the surface of my skin. "You'll have to wait for more until tonight."

Flustered, all I could do was shake my head. I swiftly finished getting dressed.

Minutes later, we were in the kitchen. I glanced over, contemplating what I'd been thinking about off and on since I'd learned Parker was his close friend.

"I'm going to talk to Parker," I announced.

Hudson drained a glass of orange juice. "He already knows we're seeing each other."

"I know, but—" I paused, gathering my thoughts. "I want him to understand that I appreciate that he cares, but I'm used to taking care of myself."

Hudson's eyes held mine. "Okay, are we going to be public about us now?"

Throughout most of my early adulthood, I had

desperately wanted to be in a committed relationship. And yet, my anxiety and expectation that things would fall apart had proven to be accurate. I'd never been public about dating anyone as a result. I feared I would jinx myself.

With Hudson, that fear ballooned. I knew the way I felt about him went far past the way I'd ever felt about anyone else. Before it had been nothing but the mist of hope. Now, my feelings were concrete. Even though I wasn't ready to speak it out loud, I knew I was already in love with him. I didn't want him to know. I was close to panic. All I could manage was a quick breath before I nodded jerkily.

Chapter Thirty-Two

STELLA

My brother studied me from across the table at Firehouse Café. "So you're telling me how it's gonna be then?"

"Yes. I appreciate that you care enough to be protective, but please don't make it awkward. This is my life."

My brother's eyes crinkled at the corners with his smile. "I won't make it awkward. It's just I know Hudson. And—"

"He told me the whole story," I interrupted.

"He did?" Parker's brows rose high.

"That you two met in detention. Everyone makes mistakes. You know my mom and our dad are back together." I rolled my eyes. "I'm happy for them, really, I am. But she didn't have the best judgment before, and neither did your dad. People grow and change, and we all learn. Just like I don't judge you, or my mom, or your dad, I don't judge Hudson. I know the man he is now."

Parker was quiet for several beats before he eventually tipped his head to the side. "Hudson's one of the best friends I ever had. We lost touch because it's kind of strange when you meet under the circumstances that we did. It was also before cell phones became ubiquitous. Even though we both spent time in Fireweed Harbor, it's not what I would call a hometown for either one of us, so we didn't cross paths after that."

"It's not really home for me either," I interjected. "My mom is there now, but we lived all over Alaska. She followed whatever guy she thought was going to give her the best life at the time. Are you worried about this?" I asked just as Janet arrived at our table with a tray. She picked up the empty plate from my finished croissant.

"About what?" Janet asked, glancing between us.

Parker eyed me uncertainly.

I decided to take the blunt approach. "Look, I'm not keeping it a secret. Hudson and I are seeing each other and Parker's my half-brother. I'm sure you've heard that from Tiffany or somebody," I said to Janet. At her nod, I continued, "He's worried about me and Hudson and wants to be protective."

Janet smiled warmly between us. "I knew all of that, except the part about Parker knowing about you and Hudson." She waggled her brows. "Stella can take care of herself, and she has plenty of friends here. We'll make sure that Hudson takes good care of her. It's sweet that you're being all older brother-ish though," she teased.

Parker sighed as he ran a hand through his hair. "I didn't know I had a sister until recently, so maybe I'm overreacting."

"You and Hudson are good friends, you should know he's a good guy," Janet pointed out.

"I do," Parker muttered. "I don't even know how to explain this."

Janet reached out, squeezing his shoulder. "You care about Stella and so do we all." Her gaze bounced to me. "I'm glad about you and Hudson. I knew he had a thing for you."

My cheeks heated as I looked up. I was relieved when Tiffany arrived, immediately making a beeline for our table. "Are you ready to meet Biscuit?"

Janet chuckled as she moved on to check on another table.

Tiffany looked so expectant and cheerful, I couldn't help but laugh. "You really want me to meet Biscuit."

She nodded vigorously, giving me a saucy grin. "I do. I mean, obviously, I love animals. I *am* the office manager at a vet clinic after all, and the rescue program is one of the things I love the most about Wes."

"Is that how you two met?" I asked.

"I'll fill you in, but we need to get going. I have a schedule," she explained. She and Parker chatted for a minute while I got my jacket on and stood. Waving goodbye to Parker, I left with her.

Outside in the parking lot, I angled toward my car, but Tiffany caught me by the elbow. "Ride with me. I'll drop you back off here."

As she drove, I repeated my question. "Is that how you and Wes met? At the rescue program?"

Tiffany snorted. "It's much more complicated than that. To make a very long story short, one of my best friends and one of his best friends got married after college. Wes and I never met until they both died in an accident. We were named joint guardians of their son."

When she stopped at an intersection, I glanced over, my eyes wide. "I'm really sorry about your friends."

Her eyes were sad. "I am too. And, thank you." She took a quick breath before continuing, "So, we became joint parents basically. We've since adopted Ross, along with the dog Wes was fostering at the time. Conveniently, we actually love each other. Wes is not a hard sell. He's totally hot."

I burst out laughing. "I'm glad you think so."

She glanced to the side. "While I don't want you to lust after my husband, surely you agree he's hot?"

I sputtered a laugh as I nodded.

"Hotshot firefighters are pretty hot in general," she added.

My mind instantly spun to Hudson. While I had an objective appreciation for Wes's looks, that was it.

"Speaking of hotshots, what's the scoop with you and Hudson?"

I contemplated her question for a few seconds. I could deny it, but we'd already had this conversation about being public. "I guess we're sort of dating. I don't know." My cheeks were burning up.

"You're roommates. I've been in that rental. Paisley and Russell used to live there. It's kind of one of those places." She circled her hand in the air.

"One of those places?" I prompted.

Tiffany slowed, her blinker clicking as she turned onto a side road. "Where you can maybe fall in love." She waggled her brows suggestively when she glanced over.

I let out a sigh. "I can't fall in love."

"Why not? It's great for your mental health if it's with the right person. Hudson seems totally solid."

I thumped my head against the back of the seat. "He does, but I have a terrible track record with relationships. I can't fall in love."

"Let's break this down," she began. She slowed to park in front of the large building straight ahead. She turned the car off and looked over at me. "Why can't you fall in love?"

I contemplated that before quickly summarizing, "I just want stability. It seems best if I find it by myself. I love my mom, a lot, but she's totally a flake and we bounced around a lot. And now, she's back with my dad and is waxing poetic about how we can all bond as a family. She texted me this morning that they want to come visit."

Tiffany's gaze was warm and understanding. "You know the story I told you about my brother discovering the other half of his family?" I nodded, wondering where this was going. "I'll keep it brief, but none of us were surprised our mom lied about Chase's father. Our mom was a nightmare. I've had years of therapy over it. She was toxic and hurtful to both of us. It doesn't sound like your mom was like that, but instability can make childhood painful. We had our dad, and he made up for everything our mom wasn't. He was and is my rock. Maybe the details are really different for you and me, but I definitely understand that what happened in your childhood might lead you to think that love won't be worth it. It is. Life can surprise you. People can surprise you. If there's one thing I figured out in my collision course with Wes, it's that you can't really tell your heart what to do. Sometimes things sneak up on you."

As I held Tiffany's gaze, tears stung my eyes. I was startled at the rush of emotion. I wasn't ready to say it out loud, or even really to admit it to myself, but a tiny part of my mind knew I was already in love with Hudson. I just didn't know how to keep my heart safe. I blinked and looked away.

Tiffany was gracious enough not to push. When I looked back at her, I asked, "But what if Hudson doesn't feel the same way?"

Tiffany's confidence was remarkable. "If it's right, he will."

I rolled my eyes. "That sounds a little woo-woo."

She leaned across the console and gave me a quick hug. "Maybe it is woo-woo," she said as she leaned back. "But I believe we find the right people that way. Now, let's go meet a cat. Biscuit will show you what true love is."

Tiffany turned out to be right on that. Biscuit was the color of a baked biscuit, a light creamy color with darker hints of gold. She was fluffy like a lioness and all she wanted was to snuggle. She curled up in my arms and began purring.

"Obviously, I'm taking her home," I announced.

Chapter Thirty-Three
HUDSON

Butter skittered across the floor in front of me as I walked in the front door. Another cat-shaped blur, almost the same color, came dashing by. I watched as the two cats raced into the kitchen and reappeared in the entryway.

Stella came walking over from the kitchen. "That's Biscuit," she offered with a smile. "I decided to adopt her. I hope it's okay."

The cats came dashing by again. "Clearly, Butter likes Biscuit," I pointed out.

Stella giggled. "As soon as I let Biscuit out, they smelled each other all over." She glanced at her watch. "This game of chase has been going on for about fifteen minutes."

I chuckled and stopped to hang up my jacket and kick off my boots. Stella's ponytail was lopsided, her curls falling down around her neck. Her eyes caught mine, and all I could think was I wanted to kiss her. So, I did.

I closed the distance between us and stopped in front of her, lifting a hand to catch one of those curls dangling along the side of her neck. "You look beautiful," I murmured as I dipped my head and dropped a kiss along the soft skin under the edge of her jaw. I was gratified at the rise of goosebumps on her skin.

On the heels of a breath, it felt like my entire body was breathing her in. My lips brushed over hers, once and again. That was all it took before I tumbled into the fire with her.

We had an unbroken record of breaking our first rule. Although I suppose it was no longer a rule. Yet, we still hadn't defined *us* more than that. A corner of my thoughts worried over this as we fell asleep a little while later. Butter and Biscuit curled up together between our feet. Even that seemed to be a clue that my heart understood and yet my mind shied away from it.

The following morning, we drove into town together since it was a weekend. Stella had a regular office job, so she actually took Saturdays off. As I drove, I felt her eyes on me.

"What is it?" I asked.

"I talked to Parker. He was worried I didn't know your history." She let out an annoyed huff.

"You guys have a similar story. I don't know why he would be so worried about that. I also pointed out that he was my brand-new brother. I'm not used to having a brother who thinks he has a say in my life, not like that. Honestly, the whole thing is annoying."

I chuckled at that. "I suppose it is. When I knew Parker when we were younger, he didn't know he had any siblings."

"We could have more," she said. "My mom texted me. Now that she and my dad have reconnected, she's all about love." Stella's sigh was resigned. "I guess they want to come to visit. I plan to ask my dad if he's aware of other siblings out there."

"When you and your mom did the DNA tests, did anyone else show up?" I asked. I slowed as I approached Main Street in the downtown area.

Glancing over, I saw Stella's curls swinging as she shook her head. "But then, you never know, Parker found me because he did a DNA test after my mom uploaded our info. These days, people should be smarter about secrets," she said dryly. "Not like I was a secret, but it's not hard for people to figure out their family history on their own now."

"No kidding. Although it doesn't sound like your dad was trying to hide things, more that—" I paused as I considered how to frame what I meant.

Stella jumped into the gap, "My dad wasn't making the best choices and, as a result, he wasn't around to be a dad for me. It sounds like he stepped up for Parker, but even then, Parker said he stayed with his aunt whenever his dad ended up in jail."

I turned into the parking area for Firehouse Café. When I stopped, Stella was looking over, her gaze was somber. "What is it?"

She shrugged. "I guess you do understand what my dad's like based on what you've shared about yours."

I smiled wryly. "I think I probably do." Impulsively, I leaned across the seat and planted a kiss on her. "I'm glad you don't think I am an awful guy because I got in trouble in high school."

Her gaze was warm as she studied me. "I think you're a pretty good guy, Hudson."

It felt as if she had stuck out her foot and my heart tripped over it, stumbling and nearly falling. I swallowed through the sudden rush of emotion.

"Let's get coffee," Stella said as she began to climb out.

I was relieved the moment passed swiftly.

A few minutes later, we reached the front of the line, and Casey greeted us. "Hi!"

Stella was eyeing the display case of baked goods while I ordered our coffees. Janet came walking out of the back. She caught my eyes, her smile wide. "You know Stella's favorite coffee," she said by way of greeting.

I managed a low laugh. My heart was still scrambling and trying to recover from its fall. I had never in my life unintentionally memorized someone's preferred food, coffee, or anything. I'd never been involved with someone long enough to reach that point.

Stella glanced over with a cheery wave.

Janet gestured toward Casey who had already started to prep our coffees. "You've met Casey, right?"

"Of course!" Stella grinned at Casey. "She makes amazing coffee."

Janet winked as she walked by. "She raises the bar for that. She's even taught me some new things."

"How do like it here now that you've been here more than a minute?" Stella asked.

Casey adjusted one of the knobs on the espresso machine. "I love it so far."

"I told you so." A teasing voice came from behind us. Maisie stopped on Stella's other side, adding, "I promised her she'd love Willow Brook."

Casey smiled between Stella and Maisie. "You did! This town is great, and this job has made it easy to settle in. It's the perfect place to get to know who's who."

Beck arrived just behind Maisie and the group expanded a little further when Parker and Griffin appeared. Parker's eyes bounced from Stella to me and back again. I was relieved for the conversation carrying on around us.

At one point after we had moved away from the

counter, Parker paused beside me. "I'm glad you told her the truth."

I held his gaze. "I don't hide my past. I respect that you have your reasons to be protective, but you know I'm not some asshole."

"I know that. Just don't hurt her."

Beck arrived at my side, taking a swallow of his coffee. "Don't hurt who?"

A dry laugh rustled in my throat. Parker replied, "Stella. They're seeing each other, and she's my sister."

Beck's brows rose as his curious gaze landed on me. "Oh, well then."

I rolled my eyes. Another guy walked over with Griffin, stopping beside Beck.

Griffin glanced around. "Guys, this is Leo." He did the introductions quickly. "He'll be starting on our crew in another few weeks."

"Why aren't you starting now?" Beck asked.

"I'm in town to deal with the paperwork, but I have to go back to finish moving," Leo explained.

"From where?" Maisie prompted.

Leo was unruffled by the curiosity. "I grew up here, but my parents moved away when I was in high school."

"Wait a sec, are you Leo Massie?" Beck prompted.

"That would be me," Leo said with a grin.

"Holy shit!" Beck's eyes widened. "You used to live next door when I was a kid."

"Beck Steele?" Leo asked.

"Hell, yeah!" Beck lifted his palm for a high five and Leo chuckled when they slapped palms.

"Oh, man, we used to have some fun together. We ran around in the woods like wild kids." Beck chuckled. "This is awesome! So, wait, where did your parents go and don't you have a sister?"

"My parents are back and forth between Juneau and here, and my sister's in grad school in Juneau," Leo explained. "That's where my mom grew up. My grandparents had some health stuff to deal with, so my parents moved to help them. When I saw this position, I decided to go for it. My parents never sold the house here and they live there when they're in town. There's a small house beside the main one, so that's where I'm staying."

"This is so cool!" Beck beamed. "Really good to have you back." He glanced around the group. "Guys, we need to go to Wildlands tonight."

When I left a few minutes later with Stella, Parker was still grumpy and I could feel his gaze practically burning a hole in my back. I told myself I wasn't going to hurt Stella, so it didn't matter.

Chapter Thirty-Four
STELLA

A few weeks later

Casey cast a dimpled smile as she handed over my coffee. "Here you go," she said in a singsong voice.

"How many customers' favorites do you have memorized now?" I teased as I took a swallow of my coffee, letting out a satisfied sigh when I lowered the cup. "This is perfect, just strong enough and not bitter."

"I'm glad to hear that. I guess I memorize favorites for anyone who comes in more than once or twice a week and usually gets the same thing. I don't really try, it becomes a habit." She reached up, tightening her ponytail, her auburn hair swinging as she released it.

"You mentioned before Alaska was on your bucket list. What do you think of it?" I asked.

"I love it so far. It feels a little cliché because lots of people say they want to come to Alaska, but I'm so glad I came. It's hard to describe how amazing it is."

"Cliché or not, Alaska *is* beautiful," I pointed out. "Do you think you'll stay?"

Casey's hazel eyes widened as she eyed me thoughtfully. "I don't know," she finally said after a long pause. "I really love it. I think the answer is yes, but—" She paused. "I'm not sure."

"Well, you'll figure it out," I said, just as Tish arrived with Phoebe.

"Hey!" Tish gave me a quick side hug.

"Hi, ladies," Casey said. "The usual for both of you?"

"Yes, please," Tish began, before correcting, "Add an extra shot of espresso to mine. I'm exhausted." Her gaze shifted to Casey. "My son is almost two years old. He has a cold and he's sleeping horribly. As a result, no one else is sleeping either."

Maisie arrived at the tail end of this comment, offering a sympathetic glance. "I love my kids, but I will never miss when they're sick. It's like an entire household project. You can't avoid it."

"And, they swap germs like a competitive sport," Phoebe offered with a sympathetic glance.

"I like my sleep, but it'll be worth losing it if I have kids, right?" I teased.

"I advise only having kids if you definitely want kids," Tish interjected. "My baby wasn't planned, but I thought about it long and hard. It's not easy."

"I work in family law," I interjected. "There are so many people who have kids when they didn't really want them. They liked the idea, but not the reality. They do keep lawyers in business, but it's so sad sometimes."

"Totally makes sense." Casey's ponytail swung as she nodded along.

"You need to come to card night," Maisie announced.

After a moment, Casey pointed toward herself. "Are you talking about me?"

"Yes!" Maisie said enthusiastically. "It's on Friday at my place this time. The kids are spending the night with Beck's mom and I told him he wasn't allowed to come home until after ten."

"You should go," I encouraged Casey when she looked uncertain.

"Are you sure?" she asked.

Tish smiled over at her. "Please. Stella and I are still pretty new to town –"

Phoebe cut in, "You've been here almost two years now."

Tish rolled her eyes. "You grew up here, Phoebe."

Phoebe nodded agreeably. "True."

"I promise, it'll be fun," I encouraged Casey. "If you want, I'll pick you up. Just let me know where."

"I ended up with this job because I'm renting an apartment from Janet." She gestured to the side. "In the building next door."

"Oh, right. Janet rents those apartments upstairs," Tish said.

"Speaking of that, do you know if the one across the hall is still available?" Maisie asked.

Casey nodded as she slid several drinks across the counter and began ringing everyone up. "Yeah, Janet said a couple moved out. Now, it's empty. I'm sure it's nice. My place is adorable and it's furnished, for the win!" She lifted one fist in the air in a mini-cheer.

"I'll pick you up, say around…?" I glanced to Maisie.

"Six," Maisie said firmly.

"Awesome! Everyone seems really nice here," Casey replied.

"Most everyone is," Janet said, hearing Casey's comment as she came through the swinging half-door that led to the kitchen. "And, you should hang out with these girls. They're all nice and they'll take care of you. Watch out though, if you have something against firefighters, they're probably gonna end up setting you up with one," she teased.

Casey's eyes widened. "I don't need to be set up

with anyone," she said, firmly enough that I assumed there was a story there.

"But firefighters are great," she added. "They save people and put out fires."

The group gradually filtered apart as we all headed back to wherever we were going. I had a few meetings this morning and planned to buckle down and study for the bar exam this afternoon. My scheduled exam date was looming in the future, and I was beyond nervous. I knew I could pass, but I was worried my anxiety would get the best of me.

I kept meaning to study in the evenings, but I often lingered with Hudson. I never expected to enjoy spending time with someone the way I did with him. There was an ease to being with him I'd never experienced with anyone else.

That night, we had another relaxing evening, eating leftover pizza and lounging in front of the TV. Biscuit and Butter snuggled together when we went to bed.

Hudson, as was his habit, gave me another shockingly good orgasm later. But I slipped up. I let my heart do the talking instead of my head. I rolled over, my chin resting on the back of my hand on his chest.

"Wow," he rasped. "You spoil me."

Like a complete fool, I went and said, "I could say the same for you. I think I love you."

The second the words were out of my mouth. I knew they were a mistake. A huge mistake.

Hudson's eyes went wide. He played it cool, but I could literally feel him withdrawing in increments, even though he didn't move.

He cleared his throat. "You're amazing," he replied.

Because *that's* exactly what someone wants to hear when they just said the *L* word.

We fell asleep together, but when I woke up, he was already gone.

There was nothing unusual about that, except he didn't wake me up to say goodbye. I told myself it was nothing.

Chapter Thirty-Five
HUDSON

Stella's words played like a broken record in my thoughts. The repetition was making me restless and irritable.

I wished the crew would get a call out to a fire. I needed something, anything, to keep me occupied. While I was mentally trying to run from my feelings, my feelings were punching me in the heart. I knew how I felt about Stella and it terrified me.

At the station, I put myself through a punishing workout. After a round of weights, I hopped on the elliptical and settled into an interval workout for a solid hour.

Parker was leaving the workout area when I walked in. I caught his gaze as he swiped a towel across his face. "Later," he said, his tone light. His smile was friendly and easygoing.

Meanwhile, my smile felt brittle, just like my heart. Parker had turned out to be prescient to worry about me hurting Stella. He would fucking kill me if he knew how panicked I was.

After I finished working out, I took a scalding hot shower and got ready to leave. It was early evening. With it being late winter, the days were getting longer. Leo was sitting in the kitchen area with Beck, Griffin, and Graham. Graham glanced over at me. "Come to Wildlands with us."

"Okay," I said immediately.

This was perfect. I didn't need to go home, I didn't need to worry about figuring out how to have any kind of interaction with Stella. Not yet.

"Are we leaving now?" I asked when I paused by the table.

"In a hurry or something?" Beck drawled, his perceptive gaze coasting over my face.

I shrugged. "I guess I'm in a hurry to eat because I'm starving."

That seemed good for Beck, although his eyes narrowed for a beat before he nodded.

"Let's roll then," Graham replied.

A short while later, we were at Wildlands. The group had expanded beyond Graham, Leo, Beck, Griffin, and me to include Cade, Jonah, Wes, and Donovan with others filtering in. We occupied two large round tables, hastily dragged together. I ended up seated between Leo and Beck with Wes and Griffin across from us.

"How's the new cat?" Wes asked after a waiter delivered the drinks to our table.

I glanced over, my blank look causing his brows to rise as he studied me. "Tiffany told me Stella brought Biscuit home. How's Butter handling it?"

Leo glanced between us. "Cats named Butter and Biscuit?"

"They're getting along great," I replied.

"Awesome." Wes grinned. "Tiffany loves being a pet matchmaker."

"How are you and Stella doing?" Griffin asked.

"Oh, we're great," I said, probably too quickly.

"Yeah? You don't sound great," Beck interjected.

Wes eyed him. "I think you missed your calling, Beck," he said dryly.

"What do you mean?" Beck countered.

"You're always grilling people on their relationships, you should've been a therapist," Wes teased. His gaze arced to Leo. "Are you single?"

"Uh, yeah," Leo replied, giving Wes the side-eye.

"Watch out, man. Beck's gonna give you the whole spiel on how great marriage and kids are. To be honest, I was skeptical, but I'm all in now," Wes replied.

Griffin lifted his hand to slap a high-five across the table. "Same here."

I took a gulp of beer, relieved when a waitress arrived at our table. I glanced up to notice it was the same woman who was also working at Firehouse Café. "Oh, hey there, Casey," I said. "You working here too?"

She smiled brightly, her ponytail swinging with her nod. "I'm only part-time here, just picking up shifts when they need someone. I see y'all are all set with the beer, but what can I get you for food?"

Wes glanced around the table. "Should we keep it simple and just get combo orders we can share?"

Casey shrugged. "Order whatever y'all want."

"How about whatever's fastest?" I interjected. "Can we start with a couple of those variety appetizer platters?"

"Absolutely." Casey's gaze circled the table, quickly counting. "There are ten of you, so maybe four platters."

"How about some of the slider platters for burgers," Beck suggested. "That should be enough."

When we nodded in collective agreement, Casey grinned. "You guys are awesome! You're making my job really easy."

"Hey, we aim to please," Beck quipped.

Casey hurried off. By the time the night rolled to a close, I knew I'd had a little too much to drink to drive myself home. As I was contemplating what to do about this, Leo happened to be walking beside me in the back hallway. "You need a ride?" he asked.

"That would probably be smart. Do you mind?"

"Of course not," he said, clapping me on the shoulder. "Just tell me where to go. Let's make sure your truck is locked up."

After I confirmed that, I followed him over to his truck. When I climbed in, I had to fumble to get my seatbelt buckled. I leaned my head back, closing my eyes for a minute, and willing the spins to stop.

"I don't usually drink that much," I mumbled as I opened my eyes and straightened, relieved to discover that I could at least see straight.

"No worries," Leo commented as he started the engine. "Where to?" he asked a moment later at the entrance to the parking lot.

"Take a left, I'm not that far away. Where are you staying in town?"

"Just a little way out of downtown. I only had one beer, so..."

We fell into silence for the drive with me offering guidance on the few turns to get to my place. Leo glanced over once he stopped in front of the house. "You good?" he asked as I began to climb out of the truck, stumbling slightly when my boot caught on a piece of gravel.

Clearing my throat, I straightened, steadying my balance. "I'm good. Appreciate the ride home."

He nodded. "Anytime. You have a ride to get to your truck in the morning?"

"I'll work it out. Thanks again."

With a wave, I closed the door and waited as he

backed up and drove away. His headlights arced across the front of the house when I began walking up the steps. I wondered if Stella was awake and kind of hoped she wasn't. At the same time, I hoped maybe she was. You see, she soothed my heart, and that fucking terrified me.

A moment later, I was standing in the kitchen. Stella finished putting a plate in the dish rack and turned to face me. She tipped her head to the side. "Are you okay?"

I stuffed my hands in my pockets. "I can't be in love," I announced.

She blinked before pain flashed in her gaze. "Okay," was all she said.

I stood there, all the while my heart felt like a jackhammer against my ribs, threatening to crack them into pieces. Maybe they would shatter just like I had shattered myself.

"That's it?" I prompted.

"Hudson, what do you expect me to say? That's not rhetorical. I told you I thought I loved you. Tonight, you show up and announce that you can't be in love. It's fine." She shook her head with a sigh. "When this all started, we were on the same page. I guess we still are. I didn't mean to catch feelings, but I think it's best that we reset."

"Reset?" A sense of panic started to churn in my chest as my heart continued battering my ribs.

"It was a mistake to let this even start. It was a

mistake for us to sleep together and I'm not talking about the sex part. I'm going to wish you a good night. The cats are asleep upstairs on my bed. Should I bring Butter down to you?"

"What? No!" I shook my head wildly.

"You don't want me to bring Butter to you?" she pressed. Her expression was flat and hard to read. I wanted to pound my fist against the wall she was building between us. It was invisible, but it felt impenetrable.

"No, I don't want you to go sleep by yourself."

Stella was quiet for several long beats while the panic continued to pound its unruly fist inside of me. "You can't be in love, and I think I am. We're going to rewind. I'm an expert at boundaries when I need them. I'm going to close the door to my stairs and go to bed. You're going to sleep downstairs. If you want Butter with you, tell me now."

I couldn't separate Butter and Biscuit. They were in love. I couldn't even handle pondering what that meant in relation to me and Stella.

My entire chest hurt and I felt a little sick. "Uh, no."

She nodded, just once, and walked past me. I had to curl my hands into fists to keep from reaching for her.

Chapter Thirty-Six
STELLA

I would never, absolutely *never*, admit to Hudson that I cried myself to sleep that night. Butter and Biscuit curled up together and mashed themselves in a single ball against my hip. The sound of their collective purring was comforting. I was relieved that I wasn't sleeping alone.

Childishly, I felt a petty joy that they picked me. It was like when you had a breakup. When you were trying to be mature and understand that shared friends wanted to maintain their connections with both of you, yet most of your friends ended up closer to you. The petty joy didn't last. I woke up alone the next day. Hudson had already left and I told myself that was for the best.

Chapter Thirty-Seven

HUDSON

A week later

Parker studied me, his gaze too perceptive for my comfort. I shifted my shoulders and drained the small bottle of water in my hand.

"What's up?" I finally asked when I tossed the empty bottle into the recycle bin a few feet away. We were in the kitchen at the fire station.

"You dumped her, didn't you?"

"What?" I knew my face gave me away because he caught me off guard. "We were never serious," I added hurriedly.

All the while, my heart literally ached. It felt as if someone had punched it hard enough to leave it bruised and battered.

"You said you wouldn't hurt her." His eyes were narrowed and his tone low.

"She's the one who called it off!" I knew I was defensive, but at least that detail was true. I wasn't about to tell Parker the entire truth.

"Is that what she's gonna tell me?" he asked with a skeptical brow raised.

Just then, Griffin came walking in. He fetched one of the electrolyte drinks out of the fridge, calling over, "Does anybody else need one?"

"I'll take one," Beck said as he approached and plunked down in a chair across from me. Next thing I knew, Jonah had joined us, along with Leo.

"What is this? A freaking meeting?" I muttered under my breath.

"Why is Parker glaring at you? I thought you guys were old friends," Beck commented.

"We were, until he dumped Stella," Parker replied.

"Oh, my God, she dumped me," I countered.

"Well, now that's fucking awkward. Aren't you renting at that duplex together?" Griffin interjected.

I rested my elbows on the table, dropping my face into my hands with a sigh. When I lifted my head, Leo caught my eyes, his gaze sympathetic and amused. "I'm sure it'll be fine," he offered.

"Romance drama," Cade commented as he sat down at the table and slid the bottles of juice to the center of the table.

Parker still didn't look pleased, but at least he didn't look like he wanted to beat my face in anymore.

Griffin looked between us. "You can't let shit like this be a problem," he pointed out.

"It won't," I said quickly. "You don't need to worry about that on my end."

I left the station that afternoon feeling disgruntled and dreading going home. The worst part of all of it was I missed Stella. I missed looking forward to seeing her, to laughing about the cats, I missed being tangled up in the darkness with her and waking up to her scent.

Her details were imprinted on my senses, the way she smelled a little tart, like the burst of flavor from a fresh berry, the way her skin was soft and warm, the way her big brown eyes widened right before she climaxed. The way her nose wrinkled a little bit when she was thinking. The sound of her fingers tapping on the table when she was studying.

When my phone rang and my dad announced he was passing through Willow Brook for the evening, I was relieved. My dad was a great distraction. I told him to meet me at Firehouse Café.

"Hey, hey!" My dad pulled me into a back-slapping hug. He felt a little frail, thinner than he used to be.

"Hey, Dad," I said, smiling as I stepped back.

This version of my dad was someone I was still

getting used to. Even though most of the reason I had made disastrous decisions when I was in high school stemmed from him, my dad had always been a loving guy, if more than a little misguided.

His smile was warm and his eyes were clear. His girlfriend, or the love of his life as he described her, was standing beside him. She smiled. They kind of matched. She had that whole peace and love vibe going, which my dad had always had, minus the drug dealing.

"Hudson!" She smiled warmly, leaning over and dusting a kiss on my cheek.

"Hey there, Laura. Good to see you."

"I'm kind of hungry," my dad said. "How's the food here?" he asked as we approached the counter.

Casey was waiting and glanced up, a smile stretching across her face. "The food here is great."

My dad grinned. "Excellent!"

"She speaks the truth, Dad," I replied just as Janet came walking through the swinging door from the back.

"Are you Hudson's father?" Janet's voice lilted up.

"I sure am. We're just passing through. Well actually, we're in Anchorage, but I came out here to see my boy." My dad beamed. I could've sworn there were tears in his eyes when he looked my way. "He's a firefighter, did you know that?"

Maybe Janet didn't know our whole history, but I could tell she sussed out the overall picture, that my dad had been there and done that and was deeply proud of me now. She cocked her head to the side, her eyes twinkling. "He isn't just a firefighter, he's a wildlands hotshot firefighter, the toughest ones in the world. You should be proud of him."

I thought my dad's face might crack wide open with his smile. "I am."

We got sandwiches and coffee, and Janet joined us for a little while. It was really good to see my dad. Despite the chaos of my childhood, he'd been making a clear effort to turn the ship around. I'd never doubted his love for me. To have him finally sort of stable was refreshing. He was sober and religiously attended Narcotics Anonymous meetings, even planning to attend a meeting when they got back to the hotel in Anchorage tonight.

A while later, I hugged him and Laura goodbye. On my way out, Janet was looping around the café with a tray as she collected dishes and tidied tables. She caught my eye and beckoned me over.

"What is it?" I asked when I stopped at her side.

"Your dad sure loves you."

My throat felt thick and my eyes pricked with tears. "He does. I love him."

She squeezed my elbow affectionately. "How are you and Stella?"

I opened my mouth to reply before snapping it shut. I realized I might be about to burst into tears if I tried to talk about my own idiocy.

Her smile faded. "What is it? Did you break that girl's heart? I don't believe you did."

I cleared my throat up, dredging up some composure. "I hope I didn't." A sigh slipped out. "I don't know how to explain it," I finally added.

Janet tipped her head to the side and studied me for a few beats. "I don't have all the answers, but I'll say this. If it's worth it, you'll stumble through and come out on your feet with her."

When I got home that night, the door up to Stella's apartment was closed and the kitchen was dark. I tried to have faith in Janet's words.

Chapter Thirty-Eight
STELLA

"Oh, honey!" My mother flung her arms around me.

When we stepped apart, her eyes were shining with tears, and I could feel my own threatening.

"I've missed you, sweetie."

"I've missed you too, Mom."

She ran one hand down my arm and smoothed the other over my hair. The man I presumed was my father was lingering at a distance, waiting by the car rental.

"Are you ready to meet him?" she asked.

I nodded. "Ready as I'll ever be."

With a smile, she slipped her hand through my elbow and walked me over to him. I didn't want to be nervous, but I was. My pulse was tumbling along unsteadily and my stomach felt a little topsy-turvy. When you have a parent just floating out there in the universe, it feels disorienting. There's so much to wonder about. My mom had never kept any secrets. She'd always been honest with me about getting pregnant young and not really being serious with my dad. When I got old enough to ask about why my dad wasn't around, she'd explained he'd been in trouble with the law.

Even at ten years old, I'd had to bite my tongue. Because, you see, maybe the guys my mom kept trying to find weren't in jail, but they weren't all that great either. A few of them had been abusive and not a single one of them had been a steady influence in my life. From what little Parker had shared, his dad was a little like my mom. Except his flakiness lent itself to dealing drugs and ending up in jail. Maybe he hadn't been so desperate for someone to save him, like my mom. Parker had assured me that he was a loving guy, and, as Parker put it, misguided and with sometimes "stupid" judgment.

I could see myself in my father when I stopped in front of him. We shared the same eyes. My dad straightened and his Adam's apple bobbed up and down when he swallowed.

"Stella," he said, my name coming out a little ragged. He cleared his throat. "It's nice to see you."

My mom's smile was so wide, I thought her face might break apart. If her entire body could smile, it would've.

I managed to draw in a slow breath. "Nice to

meet you," I finally said. "I've been thinking about it, and I know you are my dad, but I've never called anyone "dad"."

"Why don't you just call me Parks? That's what most people call me," he said easily.

"I like that." I felt the tension bundled tight in my chest start to unwind. I appreciated that he wasn't denying the awkwardness and uncertainty surrounding all this.

My mom squeezed my elbow before releasing it and clasping her hands together. "I don't want to pressure you two."

I slid my gaze to hers. "It's okay, Mom. I know that you want us all to be one big happy family inside of five minutes."

Parks's laugh was a raspy chuckle. "She sure does."

He glanced to me after he spoke. After a beat, I could tell he wasn't sure if he should've said that.

I grinned. "He knows you well, Mom."

She let out a tiny sigh, unable to stop smiling.

"So, Mom, you told me you were coming for a visit, but I don't know where you're staying, or how long you guys are going to be in town. What's the scoop?"

"We're staying at Wildlands Lodge, so I thought we could get dinner there. Parker said he could meet us, but I don't know how you feel about that," she said.

I didn't mind that at all. More than anyone, in this situation, Parker would completely understand how I felt.

"I think it sounds great. Let's go over now," I said.

All things considered, meeting my father went okay. It kind of surprised me, but he seemed like he could be really good for my mom. They had walked their meandering paths and looped back to each other. Both of them seemed more stable now. Parks was staying out of legal trouble, and my mom wasn't as desperate as she used to be. They shared a kind of worn kindness, an acceptance of where they'd been and where they were now.

My mom checked in with me about the bar exam. I eyed her. "Mom, I won't tell you the date of the exam because you'll keep asking. It's sometime in the next few months, and I'll let you know when I pass." I prayed I *would* pass.

After we finished dinner, Parker walked with me out to the parking lot. I'd sensed a little tension from him tonight. Until we stopped by my car, I chalked it up to the meeting of the parents.

He looked down at me, his eyes narrowing. "What's going on with you and Hudson?"

"Um, what did he tell you?" I hedged.

"He said *you* broke it off. I need to know if I need to kick his ass," Parker muttered.

Even though my heart thumped along, feeling

sore anytime I even thought about Hudson, Parker's comment drew a dry laugh. "I don't need anybody to kick anybody's ass on my behalf," I offered. "It's also true that I broke it off."

Parker ran a hand through his hair, scuffing the toe of his boot on the frozen gravel. "Why?"

I wasn't about to tell him I'd gotten in over my head. It wouldn't do any good for him to be angry with Hudson about it. Even though it hurt like hell, Hudson hadn't done anything wrong.

"I just did. I'm not in the right place to get serious, so it seems best to break it off." Okay, that was sort of the truth, but not really.

Parker studied me before finally shrugging. "Fine. Well, Hudson seems pretty upset about it."

I rolled my eyes. "Are you gonna kick *my* ass now on behalf of him?"

Parker's eyes widened. "Hudson's a good guy," he sputtered. He had no clue what to do with this situation.

"Look, I'm an adult, he's an adult. It'll be a little awkward for a minute and then it'll be fine. I appreciate your concern. Now, how are you feeling about the happy couple?" I gestured toward Wildlands behind us.

Parker laughed softly. "It's kind of funny. To be honest, I wish they had reconnected sooner. Even though my dad had crappy judgment, he was never a bad guy. I guess they figured it out when they were both ready. What do you think?"

I paused for a minute, collecting my thoughts. "I feel pretty much the same way. It's nice to meet your dad, or I guess, our dad. That's gonna take a little bit to get used to."

Parker gave me a hug. He squeezed tight and then let go. His hugs were almost like a physical form of punctuation.

I smiled up at him when I stepped back, my feet crunching on the frozen ground. "I'm really glad you reached out to me."

His eyes twinkled. "Same. Our parents probably would've brought us together anyway, but I'm glad we got to connect before their, uh…" He circled his hand in the air.

"Their second chance," I filled in before adding, "I'm happy for them. Obviously, you know our dad better, but life hasn't been easy on my mom. It seems like they might be in a place to be good for each other now."

"I think you might be right about that." Parker stepped back as I fished my keys out of my purse. Just as I was about to open my car door, he added, "I know you probably broke Hudson's heart, so be nice to him."

I opened my mouth to dispute his point, but that meant telling more of the story. "Of course, I'll be nice to him."

When I was in bed with the cats later, I thought about my mom and dad. I turned the word "dad" over in my mind, inspecting the idea. He *was* my dad. For years, I had jokingly referred to him as my sperm donor. While I was glad to connect with him, I knew it would take time to form a relationship. More than anything, I was really happy for my mom. I hoped things worked out for them.

Of course, the second I contemplated the idea of a relationship, Hudson came strolling into my thoughts. A sigh slipped out in the darkness. As if he sensed my distress, Butter came closer and rubbed his cheek on my shoulder. I scratched between his ears, smiling when the volume on his purring increased.

I wondered what to do about Hudson. My hormones had once again proven their epically bad track record. Even though I'd fallen for all the wrong guys when I was younger, I'd *never* let my heart get in too deep. Even though I hadn't planned to tell him I loved him the other night, my heart knew the truth.

With a disgruntled sigh, I adjusted my pillow and Butter moved away, curling against my hip beside Biscuit.

Chapter Thirty-Nine

HUDSON

After too many days of doing my damnedest to never cross paths with Stella at the house, I had to accept that Butter had clearly made his choice. Whether it was because of his love for Stella or Biscuit, he spent every night with them.

I couldn't believe it, but a cat had actually hurt my feelings. It was a relief when our crew got called out to a fire. While winter was a quiet time for fires in Alaska, our crew got called to a fishing harbor where several boats had caught fire. An even bigger fire resulted when some propane tanks near the docks exploded. Considering we had to fly across the skies of Alaska to get there, by the time we arrived, the makeshift crew of local firefighters was barely preventing the entire town from going up in flames.

I didn't have time to dwell on Stella. After a brutal first day of work, we had the fire under control. We planned to stay a few more days to establish a perimeter to protect the town and ensure none of the smoldering areas of the dock and the boats could spread the fire again.

This wasn't our usual gig. We weren't in the middle of the wilderness, but we knew how to fight and contain out of control fires. In the smaller rural villages, there was limited equipment for a big fire.

That night, we got to actually relax in the single restaurant in the tiny town. The food was simple and delicious. I leaned back in my chair, glancing around at my friends.

"This is a change of pace," I observed before taking a long drag from my water bottle.

"Gotta say, it's nice. Something other than a freeze-dried meal, or a granola bar," Nate offered dryly. Nate was flying out tomorrow. Another pilot would be picking us up in another two days.

Griffin glanced toward Nate. "Dude, you don't usually camp out for weeks like we do. This is better than nice."

Graham chuckled at his side.

"Maybe so," Nate said slowly. "But are you saying you miss having a freeze-dried dinner?"

Parker laughed. "They're not all bad. There's an art to it."

"An art?" Leo prompted.

"Sure," Parker replied. "They can be plain, or if you have a camp stove and can safely use it, you can jazz them up a little bit."

Leo's brows hitched up. "When we're out in the field this summer, I'll be looking forward to getting a jazzed-up meal from you."

"Nice that they're letting us bunk up at the school too," Nate added.

"Seriously," I replied with a nod. "Plenty of space there, not to mention hot showers." I lifted my hand to slap Graham a high five.

Conversation carried on as we relaxed. Now that we weren't in the middle of beating back that massive blaze, Stella sashayed into my thoughts. She fucking owned my spare thoughts. It was my own damned fault.

"You okay?" Leo asked from my side a little while later.

"Yeah, fine, why?"

"You're not saying much and you look like you're stressing out about something."

I snorted. "Are you a mind reader?"

"Definitely not, but you've tied that napkin into about ten different knots," he pointed out.

I let my breath out in a gust. "Missing somebody. You know how that goes."

Leo nodded slowly. "I suppose. Are we talking about Stella?"

Reflexively, I looked toward Parker, relieved to

see he was deep in conversation with Griffin.

I tried to slow the rampaging beat of my heart. Every time I thought about Stella, my heart felt like a broken drum. "She broke up with me, and I'm pretty sure it's my fault. Please do *not* fucking mention this to Parker."

"Mention what to Parker?" Graham said. He was sitting on the other side of Leo at an angle across from me from where the table curved around.

I gritted my teeth. "Nothing," I ground out.

"I know Stella dumped you, but what did you do?" Graham pressed.

"I told her I wasn't sure I could be in love," I admitted.

"With her?" Leo's brows furrowed as he winced a little.

"With anyone."

Graham's breath hissed through his teeth. "That'll do it."

"Do what?" I returned.

"Get someone to dump you, even though you're obviously in love with her," Graham said, speaking slowly, as if I had a hearing problem.

Running a hand through my hair as I leaned back in my chair, I looked between them. "I should've thought that through."

"You did her a favor, or you're an idiot," Leo said.

"A favor?"

"If you don't ever want to be serious, you did her

a favor. If she wants more, no sense in wasting time on someone like you," Leo explained.

My heart gave an achy thump. "I'm not a waste of time," I said defensively.

Graham shrugged, his head tipping to the side as he studied me. "If she wants more and that's not a possibility with you, then you would be a waste of time. Or, if it *is* a possibility with you, then you're an idiot."

My stomach started to churn uncomfortably. "Neither one of us wanted anything like that. I thought—" I cut my words off abruptly.

"Things change all the time. Maybe she meant it at the beginning, but if her feelings changed, then she did the right thing breaking it off," Leo pointed out.

I glanced between them and sighed. "I think I'm an idiot."

Chapter Forty
HUDSON

I slept restlessly that night. Every time I woke, my mind kicked around thoughts of Stella. I was a coward, at least when it came to facing my feelings for her.

I was impatient to get home, back to Willow Brook. *Back to Stella*. I needed to explain. I needed to fix things with her. As terrified as I was of how much she meant to me and what it might mean if I screwed it all up—minus the fact that I had potentially screwed it up permanently – it was more terrifying to contemplate a life where I didn't take this chance with her.

The next few days were crazy busy. It was nice to be in this tiny town on the far-flung coast of Alaska doing something a little different. Hotshot firefighter crews were designed to be on the move, to be flexible to fight fires in the deep wilderness, in the dry desert, and to protect property and towns. The small villages in Alaska had firefighters, but they didn't have the equipment and the flexibility hotshot crews did. We helped ensure the smoldering ruins were contained and had enough time to help with some repair work. We even assisted with a rescue when a polar bear cornered two kids atop an abandoned vehicle on the outskirts of town. The town organized a giant potluck hosted at the school's auditorium on the last night we were there.

I wouldn't go so far as to say I was avoiding Parker. That was pretty impossible, but I went out of my way to make sure we weren't seated together in the evenings. I didn't want him to ask me about Stella.

Just when I thought I might've skated by, Parker happened to overhear Graham. "So what are you gonna do about Stella?"

I slid my gaze to Graham's. "I'm gonna fix it."

"Fix what?" Parker asked, catching my comment as he sat down across from me.

"I'm gonna fix things with Stella, or try to," I hedged.

Parker's gaze bounced from Graham to me. "She dumped you," he pointed out.

I cleared my throat, shifting my shoulders. Maybe Graham knew better, but he threw me to the wolves here. "Hudson's not ready to admit it, but he's in love with Stella. He needs to make sure she knows that."

Parker's eyes narrowed. "Is that why she dumped you?"

I felt myself flinch and knew it gave me away.

"What the fuck?" Parker muttered. "So, technically, she dumped you, but it's because you're a coward."

I cleared my throat. "Graham said I was an idiot, so we can split the difference. I guess I'm an idiot who might be a coward."

Graham chuckled. Parker's eyes narrowed and his jaw tightened.

"Dude, cut me a little slack. This all took me by surprise. I have never—" Panic clawed in my chest and I sucked in a breath. "I've never been in love."

Graham took pity on me. "I'm here to tell you being in love is not easy."

Parker opened his mouth, as if he were about to argue the point, when Graham looked straight at him and asked, "Have *you* been in love?"

"No," Parker muttered. "But Stella's my sister."

Graham shrugged. "You can be pissed off, but give a guy a chance to get it right. I'm pretty sure he's gonna have to grovel. You can ask him to do it publicly," Graham offered dryly.

Although I felt a tiny surge of panic at that idea, I would do it.

I met Parker's eyes again, squaring my shoulders.

"I'll get down on both knees. I didn't dump her, but I wasn't ready to face my feelings. I am now. Maybe I can't fix it, but I'm sure as hell gonna try."

Parker was quiet, pressing his tongue in his cheek. "Don't break her heart."

He didn't speak to me for the rest of the night, but after he walked off, Graham rested his hand on my shoulder and gave it a squeeze. "You can handle this."

"Did you screw up with Madison?"

Graham's lips teased at the corners. "The details are different, but I wasn't ready either. By the time Madison came into my life, I'd been a single dad for so long that I couldn't even imagine something different. Madison scared the hell out of me, but we figured it out. Now that we've been together a while, I can say you have to get through a few bumpy patches before it works out. You learn how much it matters. The hard parts are what makes relationships stronger. If it's always easy..." He shrugged. "There's nothing to fight for."

Chapter Forty-One

STELLA

It annoyed me how much I missed Hudson. I was relieved that Tish called me to remind me that she was hosting card night at her place. I needed some distraction, near desperately.

I eyed Butter and Biscuit who were waiting patiently in the kitchen. They had an automated feeder, but we spoiled them with canned food. I filled their bowls and gave them each a chin scratch. "I'll be back," I said as if they understood me.

Butter twitched his tail, while Biscuit was too focused on her food to notice when I left the kitchen. I glanced out over the lake as I pulled out of the driveway. Although spring was on the way, the lake was still frozen. Growing up in Alaska, I was accustomed to spring not really happening until late May, or thereabouts.

When I arrived at Tish's place, there was plenty of food. Someone had brought two large casserole pans of homemade mac and cheese.

"Oh, my God," I said, my mouth watering just looking at it. "That looks amazing. Can I help?" I asked Tish as she set stacks of paper bowls and plates in the middle of the table.

Tonight's potluck was a hodgepodge. Sometimes we were organized enough to have a theme, but not always. In addition to the mac and cheese, Casey had brought a box of the new donuts that Janet was selling at Firehouse Café now.

Casey smiled when I sat down beside her. "I love this."

"The food?" I prompted.

"Well, the food looks great, but I feel like I'm making friends," Casey explained.

"I totally understand." I nodded vigorously. The group tonight included me, Tish, Maisie, Jasmine, Lucy, Tiffany, and Madison so far. With Graham's crew out, that meant many of us were quietly keeping worry at bay about firefighters we loved.

"Do you miss Hudson?" Madison asked.

I missed Hudson to the point my heart stung from the pain of it. And yet, I hadn't really talked about our breakup. I took a shaky breath as I nodded.

Madison's eyes narrowed. I had come to really

like Madison. Although her beauty was intimidating at first, she was a sensitive, kind friend.

"What is it?" she pressed. "We all miss our guys when they're gone, but it seems like there's something else going on."

For a beat, I thought I could hold it together, that I could play this off. Instead, I burst into tears. Tish curled her arm around my shoulders, and the whole story spilled out.

I finished with, "And, like an idiot, I don't even know if I love Hudson, but I said I thought I did and it freaked him out. There's a reason I don't do relationships."

"I don't do them either, but I'm wondering if you have a better reason than me," Casey chimed in.

"It's nothing major. Just that I don't have the best judgment, or my hormones don't," I replied, my shoulders sagging with a sigh.

"Hormones generally have great judgment," Amelia interjected dryly as she sat down at the table.

"Hudson seems like a really good guy," Tish offered softly from my side.

I cleared my throat. "My mom takes wearing her heart on her sleeve too far. It's like a competitive sport for her. I spent my childhood watching her desperately fall for one guy after another who didn't want anything serious, or were total assholes. I promised myself I would never let myself end up in that position."

Madison studied me from across the table. "You don't sound desperate for Hudson. You totally have it together. You just finished law school."

Maisie's curls bounced with her nod. "You are badass."

My heart pounded along unsteadily. "I am?"

Tish nudged me with her shoulder. "Remember when we met last year? My life was a hot mess."

"It was not!" I insisted.

"Maybe that's how it looked from the outside, but—" She shrugged. "It didn't feel like that to me at all. My point is you might feel like you don't have it together, but you're doing better than you think."

Madison chimed in, "You should've seen me when I ended up here. I was broke. All I had was my dog, my car, and the place my grandfather left me. That's it."

"Really?" I squeaked.

"Really," Madison said. "Most of us forget to consider that the way it looks on the outside probably isn't how it feels on the inside."

I took a shaky breath.

"Some people are just better at making it seem like they totally have it figured out. I don't totally have it figured out, but being a dispatcher has taught me a lot. It kind of sharpens moments and perspective," Maisie offered. "But back to Hudson, maybe talk to him again. I don't know if you love him. Only you know the answer to that, but it's possible you overreacted," she said carefully.

I rolled my eyes as a laugh rustled in my throat. "Maybe."

Tish squeezed me again. "Mac and cheese usually makes things better, so eat some. When the guys get back, maybe you can have a conversation with Hudson. I'm not saying it will all work out, but my guess is—"

Several phones rang, chimed, and buzzed in rapid succession. Madison glanced down at her phone screen. "It's Graham, let me get the update." She hurried away from the table.

Moments later, she returned. "They're flying back tomorrow." Her gaze bounced to me. "Graham said Hudson feels like an idiot."

"Really?" I felt ridiculous, but that gave me a little sprout of hope inside.

"Really," Madison said as she sat down.

"I probably shouldn't be happy about that," I added, feeling a little sheepish.

"Feel happy," Maisie said. "He should feel like an idiot."

I drew in a slow breath. As conversation moved along, I pondered my heart. I knew I loved Hudson. I didn't know if it was going to work out, but it was important for me to actually communicate with him about it.

The following morning, I woke early. I was meeting my mom and Parks for coffee. I was adjusting to thinking of him as my dad, but calling him Parks suited us both.

As we were walking out after getting coffee, they were planning another visit to Willow Brook in the summer. I smiled between them. "It'll be good to see you both again. I'm sorry Parker had to leave while you were visiting."

Parks smiled widely. "It's his job." His pride about Parker was endearing.

When Parks slipped back inside to use the restroom, my mom tipped her head to the side. "Are you ready for your exam?"

"Hope so," I said, not wanting to dwell and let my anxiety tie me up in knots.

She reached for both of my hands when we stopped beside my car. "How do you feel about your dad?"

I paused, taking stock inside. "I'm glad to meet him. I know I technically met him before, but I don't remember. I'm glad he's doing better. I'm also glad you two seem to be reconnecting. I know that's something you've always wanted."

My mom was quiet for a moment, her eyes shining with tears. She squeezed my hands hard before releasing them and pulling me into one of her fierce hugs. When she stepped back, she brushed her hands over my shoulders. "I love you."

"I love you too, Mom."

Parks had returned and looked at me with his brow furrowed. "Are we ready for a hug?"

I studied him. His face was weathered and his eyes were warm. I saw the flicker of uncertainty there. I knew he'd scraped by most of his life. He'd gotten sober and was trying to keep his life together. I knew that was more than challenging for anyone.

Emotion tightened in my throat as I smiled. "Of course."

He gave me a quick hug, his embrace firm. When we stepped apart, my heart felt squeezed tight. "I'm glad you both came to visit. Parker's supposed to be back later today, you know?"

Parks nodded. "We have to catch our flight. He knows that. We'll see him next time."

I watched as they drove away before I climbed back in my car to go home. I planned to study this morning before I went to the office this afternoon.

When I got home, I decided to let the cats out on the porch. Hudson already had a habit of doing that with Butter because he liked to watch things. I got my laptop set up at the kitchen counter and was deep into reviewing an entire section of my exam prep when Butter began meowing. He was the more vocal of the two. I got up to let him in, but he wasn't by the door. He was sitting on the railing looking down, and there was no sign of Biscuit.

When I looked beyond the railing, I could see her bounding bravely through the snow toward the edge of the lake.

"Biscuit!" I exclaimed.

She ignored me. Scrambling, I scooped Butter off the railing and carried him inside.

I raced into the entry area, stuffing my feet into my boots and flinging a jacket on before running outside to the back of the house. By the time I got to the backyard, Biscuit had walked out onto the ice and was peering into an ice fishing hole someone had used earlier in the winter.

I wasn't thinking about the possibility that it was almost spring and the ice was getting thinner. My mind was solely focused on making sure Biscuit was safe.

I kept calling her name, which was pointless. Maybe some cats came when they were called, but Biscuit wasn't one of those cats. I stepped out onto the edge of the ice.

Biscuit finally looked my way and began to walk toward me. I heard a sharp snapping sound under my feet before the ice broke open abruptly.

My mind blanked at the shock of the icy water and my breath ceased in my lungs.

Chapter Forty-Two
HUDSON

I was impatient to see Stella, but I knew she might be at work. After we landed, I tossed my gear in my locker and hurried out to my truck. I drove straight to her office, but her car wasn't there.

Uncertain where to look for her, I figured I might as well try home next. She hadn't responded to my texts. When I saw her car at the house, my heartbeat began kicking along faster and faster.

"Stella!" I called as I walked inside.

There was no sign of her in the kitchen, although her laptop was open on the counter beside the notebook she usually had out when she was studying. Butter twined around my ankles, but there was no sign of Biscuit.

The doorway to Stella's apartment was open, so I called up to her. When she didn't reply, I jogged up the stairs. Still no Stella or Biscuit. Worry started to rumble inside.

"What the hell?" I muttered to myself as I jogged back down the stairs. Butter had stationed himself beside the doorway onto the deck and was looking at me expectantly.

When I opened the door to let him out, I saw Stella in the lake.

For a split second, I contemplated barreling through the doors and jumping off the deck. But even with a good cushion of snow, I could hurt myself with that landing. Spinning around, I bolted out of the house, shedding my jacket as I raced to my truck. I grabbed the rope I always kept in the back and kept on hustling around to the back of the house. By the time I reached the edge of the pond, Stella's elbows were resting on the edge of the ice where she'd fallen through.

"Stella!"

Her head whipped up. "Hudson!"

She was ten feet or so from the edge of the shore. Biscuit, who I presumed was the reason Stella had fallen through the ice, had retreated to safer ground in the snow near the edge of the ice.

I wanted to break through the ice and rescue Stella, but it was just far enough I wasn't sure that was a wise call. I held her gaze. "Stella, can you listen to me?"

She nodded, and worry reverberated through me to see how much she was shivering.

"This may sound counterintuitive, but I want you to kick the ice up behind your feet. We want your legs to be able to float upward. That will help you to slide forward gradually instead of pushing your weight up in one place."

Stella shifted, and a few seconds later, the ice broke behind her after she kicked and her feet floated to the surface. "Okay now, try to slide your chest up onto the edge of the ice."

The ice appeared thick enough to hold her, but I didn't know. Ice could be tricky. There were always thinner and thicker areas, especially when the weather started to warm up.

"Take it nice and slow," I called out as she gradually eased her chest onto the ice. "Worst case scenario I'm gonna break through and get you, but this is the safer option."

It took all my restraint not to do more. While keeping my eyes on her, I knotted the rope around my waist and checked the sturdy handle on the other end. "I'm gonna throw this to you. Just grab ahold of the handle."

I tossed it, breathing a silent sigh of relief when it landed right in front of her. She curled one hand around the handle.

"Okay, perfect. Now, keep sliding onto the ice."

Although I could hear the subtle cracks from her weight, the ice in front of her was holding so far.

Stella was all the way onto the ice by now, still keeping a grip on the rope handle. With me talking her through it, she carefully inched forward. I kept a little slack in the rope and tightened it incrementally as she got closer and closer to the edge of the shoreline.

Biscuit waited beside me, watching Stella. All the while, I could hear the thud of my heartbeat rushing in my ears, and tried to keep my focus. It was one thing to stay focused when you were rescuing someone you didn't know. It was something else altogether when you were rescuing someone you loved. I loved Stella. That knowledge rang like a bell inside, the echo of it reverberating in my heart.

When she was about two feet away from the shoreline, I finally leaned down and reached for her shoulders, sliding her all the way onto the snow. Once I knew she was completely clear of the ice and on solid and snowy ground, I knelt down and wrapped her in my arms.

She was wet and shivering so hard I could feel it in my bones.

"I love you, Stella," I murmured into her hair.

She lifted her head. Her teeth chattered. "I-I lo-o-ve y-y-you too."

"There's a lot more I need to say, but we need to

get you inside. We might need to take you to the hospital." I stood and lifted her into my arms.

"I can walk," she insisted.

I wanted to argue the point, but the snow was almost two feet deep and starting to soften, so it was a slog to walk through. I eased her down, keeping a firm hold around her waist as we slowly made our way to the front of the house. Biscuit leaped along through the snow beside us.

"Did you come out here to get Biscuit?" I asked.

The sound of Stella's teeth chattering when she nodded twisted my heart painfully.

It felt like forever later, but it was maybe two minutes before we walked through the front door. When we stopped inside the entryway, Stella looked up at me.

My brain felt filled with static. Emotion rose like a wave cresting inside and my throat felt thick. I forced myself to focus. "We need to get you warm. Shower," I stated.

We needed to get her out of her sopping-wet clothes. I stripped her down swiftly, leaving everything in a pile in the entryway. Biscuit had followed us inside and scampered into the kitchen with Butter. I hustled Stella upstairs into her apartment and to the bathroom. She didn't hesitate and let out a deep sigh when she stepped into the warm shower.

"I'm warm," she said through the water a few moments later.

"You're staying in for a few minutes," I insisted.

There was nothing sexual about it in this moment, but I needed to be close to her. I stripped out of my own clothes and stepped into the shower behind her, curling my arms around her and simply holding her.

A little while later, Stella was dressed in a fluffy pair of fleece pants, fuzzy socks, and an oversized fleece top. I'd ordered pizza to be delivered. Stella's hands were curled around a mug of steaming hot tea. She was sitting on the couch, watching as I carried plates over to the coffee table in front of her. The cats were flanking her. I didn't know how to read a cat's mind, but I was pretty sure Biscuit realized that she might've been responsible for the chain of events that led to Stella falling through the ice. She wouldn't leave Stella's side.

When the doorbell rang, I snagged my wallet off the counter and walked quickly out to the entryway. When I swung the door open, Casey from the café was there.

"Hey, Casey," I said. "Aside from Firehouse Café and Wildlands, you also work for Alpenglow Pizza now?"

She grinned. "I switched from Wildlands to this.

I don't like those late hours. Just so you know, there is so much pepperoni on this pizza I almost stole it from you," she teased.

I chuckled, handing her a generous tip. "I don't believe there's such a thing as too much pepperoni."

"There isn't. Tell Stella I said hi," she said in a singsong voice as she jogged off the porch to her car.

When I walked back up to the living room, Stella asked, "Who was that?"

"Casey from Firehouse Café. I guess she started doing pizza delivery instead of working at Wildlands. She said hi."

Stella smiled as she set her mug on the coffee table. "I like Casey. I hope she stays in Willow Brook."

I put the pizza on the coffee table, walking back down to the kitchen to grab some napkins. "Silverware?" I yelled up.

"Nope. People who use silverware for pizza are savages."

I chuckled as I sat down beside her and handed her a napkin. She was already sliding a piece of pizza onto a plate. She closed her eyes and let out a moan as she took a bite.

It was mid-afternoon and only an hour or so had passed since I'd gotten home to find Stella in the lake. I'd lost sense of time. For the first time since, my body could focus on something other than sheer fear and making sure Stella was safe. When she moaned, I heard that sound in every cell.

After we ate, Stella leaned back against the cushions with a satisfied sigh. "I don't think I'm going to let Biscuit out on the porch ever again."

I eyed Biscuit. "I'm questioning if we should keep her," I offered dryly.

Stella's eyes went wide and her mouth dropped open in mock outrage. "You'd better be joking."

"Obviously. Butter would be devastated without her. So, what happened?"

Stella idly stroked Biscuit. "I let them out on the porch. They've always been fine out there. Butter started meowing, and when I got up to let him in, Biscuit wasn't there. I looked over the railing and she was already walking out on the lake."

I glanced at Biscuit who was purring away at Stella's side. My mind kept replaying the picture of Stella in the icy water. I had to forcefully kick the memory away. She was safe now.

On the heels of a breath, I cleared my throat. "Okay, no more porch."

"Or, we put up some kind of barrier that keeps them from jumping or climbing down," she said.

"I'll think on it and see if we can come up with something."

Stella's eyes met mine, big and brown, with her blond curls tumbling around her shoulders.

"I missed you." My words slipped out before I could think about them.

It was the simple truth. I'd already said the hard part.

She tipped her head to the side, lifting her hand to tuck a loose curl behind her ear. She was pink-cheeked and fresh-looking. "I missed you too. But I missed you before you went away." She blinked, looking at me uncertainly. "I think maybe I overreacted."

"What do you mean?" I pressed.

"When I broke up with you. My words got ahead of me," she explained.

"It wasn't you. I panicked because I love you. I was scared to even think about it, much less tell you." Saying that aloud was a relief. My heart started to loosen. It felt as if I'd been clenching a fist around it for years, holding on so tight that it hurt. I'd been afraid to let go.

"I guess we were both afraid," she said slowly. "What do we do now?"

"I need to stop being an idiot. Leo told me that I had either done you a favor, or I was an idiot." I laughed softly as I recalled his point.

"A favor?"

"By not wasting your time if I didn't want more. I was the idiot because I was a coward and didn't know how to tell you how much you meant to me."

Stella pressed her lips together to keep from laughing. I reached for her hand and laced my fingers through it. "You can laugh. It hurt to hear it, but Leo was just pointing out the obvious. And then, Parker told me again he would kick my ass if I hurt you."

Chapter Forty-Three
STELLA

I looked over at Hudson, my heart feeling warm and almost soft inside my chest. Oh, that old anxiety was still churning, spinning around it like a storm dying down. I was relieved to be honest about my feelings and deeply relieved not to be alone in them.

"What do you want?" As soon as my question slipped out, I wanted to snatch it back, to hold it tight inside.

This was always my folly, wishing someone would want what I wanted. And now, it mattered more than it had *ever* mattered. Because I loved Hudson. He was more than just an idea. He was living and breathing and occupied the whole of my heart.

I watched as his shoulders rose with a deep breath. His eyes stayed locked to mine, his gaze warm and focused.

"I want with you what I was always afraid to want with anyone. The whole thing. One day at a time, but knowing that each of those days you're walking this winding path of life with me. I want to come home and make dinner with you. I want to get pizza with too much pepperoni even though too much pepperoni is impossible." His lips quirked at the corners. "When I miss you, I want to know I'm coming home to you. When you need me, I want to be there. Although, please don't ever step out on a frozen lake ever again in your life. I nearly had a heart attack when I saw you out there."

My throat felt tight and tears stung my eyes.

"What do you want?" he asked, his words barely above a whisper.

"All of that," I finally managed to say.

"Don't cry." He lifted his hand to swipe away the tear that splashed onto my cheek.

I stopped petting the cats long enough to brush my fingers across both of my cheeks. "They're happy tears, overwhelmed tears. They're not sad tears. I promise." I took a shaky breath. "We can tell Parker he doesn't have to kick anybody's ass."

Hudson's cell phone vibrated where it sat on the coffee table. He ignored it. I cleared my throat. "You should check that," I said when it kept ringing.

He lifted it to glance at the screen. "It's your freaking brother. He's probably calling to check on me and make sure I'm not still being an idiot."

I burst out laughing at that. "For what it's worth, I told him I broke up with you, but I didn't give him any more information than that."

"It was kind of my fault, or at least I think it was," Hudson said quickly.

I rolled my eyes. "It was both of us." The phone continued to ring impatiently. "Answer the phone, or I will," I added.

Hudson released my hand and slid his thumb across the screen, tapping to put it on speaker immediately. "Parker, you're on speaker. It's me and Stella."

My brother's tone was skeptical. "Really?"

"Hey, Parker, it's Stella. You don't need to lecture Hudson again, or kick anybody's ass. I understand you want to blame this whole thing on Hudson, but it was both of us. We're all good now."

"Are you sure?" Parker pressed.

Hudson glared at the phone. "We're sure. I told her I love her, I want it all with her. What else do you need to back the hell off?"

Before Parker could answer, I cut in, "Let me remind you, I'm a grown woman and I can take care of myself. I appreciate that you care, but please don't worry about me."

Parker grumbled something before muttering, "Fine. I just want you to be okay, Stella."

"I am okay!" I insisted. "Was there something else you needed?"

Parker finally chuckled. "Nope. I'm sure I'll see you both soon."

Hudson double-checked to make sure the call had ended and tapped to close the screen before setting his phone back on the table. "I could handle it if he wanted to beat me up, but I'm glad it's not necessary." He paused, his eyes lingering on mine. "So, what are we gonna do for the rest of the day?"

We ended up having the best kind of day, mostly because we didn't do much of anything. I actually felt good enough to try to start working in the afternoon, but Hudson insisted that I had to recover. When it started to get dark in the evening, I studied a little for my bar exam while he problem-solved options for the back porch to keep the cats safe out there.

That night, we watched TV. Much as I had missed Hudson, all he wanted to do was snuggle. I was ready for a lot more than snuggling.

All that to say, having him home was the absolute best part. I savored every moment of his presence. We fell asleep upstairs with Butter and Biscuit snuggled up at the foot of the bed. As I was drifting off, Hudson murmured into my hair, "I'm trying not to take it personally that I think the cats like you better than me."

I giggled. "You've been away."

"They were sleeping up here even before I was gone."

I rose up on an elbow, looking at him in the darkness. "That's because you usually slept up here. It's what they're used to."

He smoothed a hand over my hair. The last thing I remembered was falling asleep to the sound of his heart beating where my cheek rested on his chest.

It was still dark when I came awake. For a moment, I was confused. Mostly because I'd spent the last few weeks sleeping restlessly and feeling lonely. When I came awake now, I felt warm all over. As soon as my body and brain cataloged that Hudson was spooned behind me, a sense of contentment gusted through me like a warm breeze on a summer night. It felt as if my whole body was smiling. I was just so happy he was home with me.

I didn't realize I had wiggled my bottom until I felt the hard press of his arousal against me. His voice was raspy when he spoke, "You can ignore that. I just woke up and apparently my body has an opinion."

"What if I don't want to?" I whispered back, becoming aware of my own body's unconscious reaction to him. My arousal was already slick between my thighs, and my nipples tightened when his palm caressed over my belly.

He cleared his throat, shifting to press a kiss on

the inside of my neck, right above the curve of my shoulder. Goosebumps chased over my skin with a trembling shiver.

"You can still ignore it," he repeated.

I decided to make my feelings clear and wiggled my bottom firmly against him. I tugged his hand down between my thighs. I was wearing panties, but there was no doubt at the state of the damp cotton.

"Stella..." he rasped.

"I missed you." I felt the ache of desire for him in my bones. I needed to assuage it by losing myself in him. "Hudson..." My voice contained a plea. I turned to press a kiss on his jaw.

In the darkness, a quiet time where it felt like our intimacy was a shimmering curtain protecting us from the rest of the world, we made sleepy love. Although it felt as if we were almost in a trance, it was also a little rushed and fumbled. Once he buried his fingers between my thighs and discovered I was dripping wet, he dragged my panties down my legs and kicked off his briefs. With a subtle nudge of his hips, he filled me from behind. We rocked together. My climax spiraled rapidly. Just when I was about to beg, he slid his hand down over the curve of my belly again and teased his fingers just where I needed it.

He knew my body, and I knew his. He trembled all over seconds before I felt the heat of his release filling me. He held me close, staying spooned behind me. I could feel the beat of his heart between my shoulder blades. When he dusted a kiss on the side of my neck, my lips curved into a smile. The next few moments were quiet. It felt as if we were simply absorbing each other. Our bodies communicating. *I missed you. I love you.*

Butter broke through our reverie when he leaped on the bed and meowed loudly. I could feel the rumble of Hudson's laughter through my entire body. "I forgot he's an early riser."

"I'll feed him," I said.

Butter was demanding when it came to food. Even though we left dry food out for him, he liked fresh food in the morning.

"You don't have to, I will," Hudson replied.

I opened my eyes and glanced at the clock on the nightstand. "It's almost five-thirty. I'm usually up by now anyway."

We got up together. Before I could make my way down to the kitchen, Hudson caught my hand. "Shower."

We took a quick shower together, and Hudson drew circles through the soap rolling down my back when I was rinsing the shampoo out of my hair. A short while later, he was feeding the cats and I got coffee ready.

When I turned around to see him talking to Butter, my heart felt like it might beat its way out of my chest. He was having a one-way conversation with a cat, and I loved it. I could do this for the rest of my life.

Chapter Forty-Four
HUDSON

A month later

"What'll it be?" Janet asked from behind the register.

"Huh?" I was distracted, utterly, by Stella, I hadn't noticed that the customers in front of us had already been served.

Janet drummed her fingertips on the counter, her smile sly. "I assume you were standing in line because you wanted some coffee, or something to eat?"

Casey appeared through the swinging door from the back, giggling a little when she saw the look on my face. She smiled toward Janet. "Hudson is whipped."

I heard someone approaching from behind and

glanced over to see Parker. The expression on his face was muddled, a combination of annoyed, good-natured horror, and humor. Just to get him back a little for threatening to kick my ass, I looked at Casey, smiling widely. "I am completely whipped and proud of it." Holding Stella's hand, I leaned down and gave her a lingering kiss. Her cheeks were pink by the time I lifted my head.

"Oh, for fuck's sake," Parker muttered. "You're holding up the line. You've made your point. You and Stella are doing great, and I'm happy for you."

When Stella glanced over at Parker, the flush on her cheeks deepened and a hint of annoyance flashed in her eyes. They were still getting adjusted to their newfound sibling relationship. They got along pretty well, but Stella's independent streak was strong, and she didn't appreciate Parker trying to protect her.

Casey grinned. "Take all the time you need."

"Actually, please don't," Janet said. "There's a group coming in right now." The bell chimed above the door and a cluster of tourists came walking in.

We ordered and I covered Parker's coffee. Janet chatted with us as she made our drinks. When Parker stepped away to use the restroom, she smiled between us. "I am happy for you two. Remember, let the good stuff be your shining star. Don't let the daily annoyances of life get in the way."

Beck happened to be approaching and caught

Janet's last comment. His smile was wide as he looked amongst us. "Exactly. For example, Maisie didn't do the dishes last night. I'm totally over it."

Maisie was right behind him and stopped at his side, elbowing him hard. "Last night was *your* night to do the dishes. I'm totally over it," she said tartly.

For all of the jokes about Beck being nosy, which he was, and often offering unsolicited advice on relationships, he was a happy guy. When Beck looked down at Maisie, they laughed together before he gave her a lingering kiss.

Janet glanced over. "Take their advice. They've got it figured out."

Griffin and Tish were approaching with Tiffany and Wes. "Or them," Maisie said.

"Or who?" Tish asked as she stopped beside Maisie.

"You have your relationship figured out," Maisie said with a shrug.

"Well, most of the time," Tish offered dryly as she glanced askance at Griffin.

"What?" Griffin asked, his eyes, and his brows hitching up.

"You forgot the diaper bag. I'm over it," Tish replied with a shrug.

Griffin burst out laughing. "That's why I keep an extra one in your car."

We had coffee and breakfast with friends. On my way to the restroom, Graham and Madison were walking in. Leo arrived, unaccompanied, and Beck narrowed his eyes as he studied him.

"Why are you looking at me like that?" Leo asked.

"No reason," Beck said quickly.

Leo glanced around. "Am I the only single guy here?" he asked under his breath to Griffin, who had stopped beside him.

"You're definitely not the only single guy who's a firefighter," Griffin replied with a grin.

Leo let out a breath. "Good to know."

"Why is that good?" Casey asked, before adding, "What can I get you?"

Leo's gaze lifted to hers as he shrugged. "No reason."

Beck bumped him with his shoulder. "Don't worry, man, when you're ready to settle down, I'm your guy."

"My guy? That's cool, but I thought you were married." Leo looked genuinely befuddled.

Griffin chuckled. "If you haven't figured it out, Beck is nosy."

Leo rolled his eyes. "Oh, I figured that out."

Stella was saying something to Madison at the table when I sat down beside her. I couldn't resist and leaned over to press a kiss on her cheek. When she smiled at me, my heart tripped and stumbled. She did that to me, constantly knocking me off-balance emotionally. I didn't mind because she always caught me.

"What is it?" she asked when she looked up at me.

"I'm really glad you ran over my crutches."

Her cheeks flushed pink. "I'm really glad you rescued me from that silly fire."

"Anytime."

EPILOGUE

Casey Houston

I adjusted the knobs on the espresso machine, whipping through one drink after another. Even though I'd ended up in Willow Brook, Alaska because I was running away, literally, this was a great job. Firehouse Café was adorable, my boss was awesome, and I had a sweet little apartment next door.

I finished serving the last drink from this little cluster of customers and began tidying up. I always used the small lulls here to keep things at a baseline. Chaos could ensue if I didn't. Maybe a full three minutes passed before the bell jingled above the door. I glanced up to see one of the firefighters walking in. With four hotshot crews based out of Willow Brook, there were *a lot* of firefighters in this town. Not a single day went by without seeing at least five firefighters. That was the minimum. I had actually counted a few times.

In this case, the firefighter in question was Leo Massey. Leo bordered on ridiculously sexy. He had dark gold hair, kind of like a lion. I figured it suited him since his name was Leo. Paired with that golden hair were his hazel eyes, mostly green with flecks of gold in them. All matters were made worse with a body designed to melt me. He was beyond fit and didn't even seem to know it.

"Hey," he said when he stopped in front of the counter.

"Hi, Leo!" I squeaked. Because, of course, I squeaked around him.

I could usually play it cool, but not with Leo. I silently sighed. I did *not* need to be crushing on anyone, much less this guy.

Before I could say anything else, a whole group of firefighters came in. I almost let out a giant sigh of relief. I could handle them in groups, especially when Leo was here. He was the only one who got to me.

They called out a few hellos as they clustered around Leo.

"Hey," I pointed at them one by one as I replied, "Griffin, Hudson, Graham, Levi, and..."

"Beck," said Beck as he approached last.

"As if I would forget you, Beck," I teased.

I got busy making the coffees, relieved when

more customers came in, including Stella, who was one of my first friends here and had introduced me to pretty much everybody else I knew in town.

Her curls bounced when she stopped beside Hudson and slipped her hand through his elbow. He gave her a lingering kiss. Her cheeks were pink when he lifted his head.

"Lighten up on the PDA," Beck teased.

Hudson shrugged. "I don't care."

Madison, who was married to Graham, smiled indulgently between Stella and Hudson. "They're still fresh in love. Let them have their PDA."

The group began exchanging quips and chatting. Once I had everything ready, Beck called out, "I'm paying!" as he scooped up the tray of coffees.

My eyes were drawn like a magnet to Leo as he walked out with the others. I tried not to notice how broad his shoulders were. I busied myself with wiping the counter.

Stella stopped by the register on her way out. "I need some donuts!" she shout-whispered.

"Why are we whispering?" I asked in an exaggerated whisper.

Stella giggled just as Hudson stopped beside her. "What's so funny?" He smoothed his hand down her back, curling his arm around her waist.

She smiled at him, her cheeks flushed pink. "I'm bringing donuts to the office."

"That's just smart," he teased. "In fact—" He

glanced to me. "I'll take a box of donuts. Are there enough?"

Janet had only recently added donuts to her menu. They were as close to heaven as I'd ever had for donuts.

"We have enough for two boxes. The firefighters are gonna love you," I said with a wink at Hudson.

He flashed a grin. "Honestly, it's a little selfish on my part. I'll eat two on the way back to the station."

I laughed. "Variety box for both of you?"

When they nodded, I spun away, pushing through the swinging half-door into the kitchen. Janet was bustling around and glanced over.

"I need two variety boxes of donuts," I said.

"You got it. Your timing is perfect." Janet reached into one of the rolling cases the donuts were stored in and fetched two boxes. "These are selling out every day. I'm gonna have to tell Luna we need more."

"Thank you." I took the boxes from her, adding, "Pretty sure we can sell however many Luna can make."

When I walked back out front, Hudson was looking down at Stella, his eyes practically beaming love as she said something. He dipped his head a little and gave her a lingering kiss. It felt as if I'd interrupted a deeply private moment. They were in a coffee shop in the middle of downtown Willow Brook with most of the tables full, but still.

I was relieved when he lifted his head and immediately glanced over, his eyes landing on the boxes in my hands. "My mouth is already watering."

I laughed softly as I handed the boxes over.

"I'll get them both," Hudson offered.

Stella elbowed him in the side. "No, this is work for me. You can get yours."

"It's not covered by your work for me?" he teased.

Stella waggled her brows. "I'm a lawyer. Getting a box of donuts for my fiancé's job definitely doesn't fall under a work expense."

"If it keeps you happy and means you have a more productive day at work, I think it's a work expense," I chimed in.

A moment later, I watched as they walked out holding hands. I loved *love*. But I was pretty sure it wasn't in the cards for me.

My day rolled by, busy as ever. It was early evening when I was getting ready to close up. The café was empty, and I had all the chairs up on the tables as I approached the front door to lock up. I was looking down as I walked to the door, stepping carefully since I'd just mopped the floor. When I glanced up, the door was opening and Leo was walking in.

"Whoa, are you closing?" he asked, stopping before he walked all the way inside.

"Yeah, but if you need something I can get it," I offered.

No matter the situation, I tried to please everyone. I was too flummoxed at his unexpected presence to think clearly.

"I was hoping for another coffee," he said.

"Coming right up." I gestured him through the door. "Let me lock up behind you. I just mopped, so walk slowly." I made my way back around the counter.

"Thanks for the warning," Leo said.

Sweet hell, even his voice was sexy. It was low with a smooth rumble to it. My belly did a little shimmy and twist. I cleared my throat as I looked at him from behind the counter. "Your usual?"

"Do you know my usual?" he countered, a gleam in his eyes.

"If you come in more than once a week, I know your usual. You usually get the house coffee, extra strong with a shot of espresso in it. Nothing else. Your favorite food is either a plain donut or the ham braided twist."

His brows hitched up as he let out a low whistle. "Points for that. I'll just take a coffee, no need for you to do anything else."

"Donuts are all gone for the day, they've been gone since noon, but I do have one twist left." I gestured to the display case. "I was just about to put the leftover stuff in the back."

"I can have one now?"

"Of course."

He grinned. "I'll take it."

I was relieved I could move pretty much on autopilot. Within minutes, I handed over his coffee and the small bakery bag. He insisted on paying and giving me a generous tip. Normally, I could chat casually with regular customers, but being alone with Leo tied my tongue into a tangle.

I was mentally patting myself on the back for not doing or saying anything stupid, but it all went sideways when I went to unlock the door. The floor was still damp. I heard the slip of a shoe on the floor as he reached for the door handle with me right on his heels. He had his coffee in one hand and the pastry bag in the other.

Coffee splattered down the front of my shirt, completely soaking it. "Oh!" I jumped back.

"Oh, shit, I'm sorry, Casey," Leo said as he straightened from slipping, looking horrified.

We both looked down at my shirt. I usually wore tank tops when I was working. It got hot in here with running between the kitchen area and the front. My top was soaked and clung to my chest. My cheeks were burning hot when I looked back up at Leo.

LEO

My eyes were stuck. Casey stood in front of me with her top drenched by the coffee I'd pretty much dumped on her. Her breasts were outlined perfectly. As I stared, her nipples puckered through the cotton. I mentally scrambled and dragged my eyes up to find her staring back at me. Her cheeks were adorably pink and her eyes wide.

"I am *so* sorry," I said hurriedly.

"It's okay!" She spun around, practically sprinting across the café.

The floor was still damp. She slowed just as one of her shoes began to slide on the floor. She was by the counter at this point and reached out, her hand catching it just before her feet began to skid again.

I followed, setting my now mostly empty cup of coffee on the counter with my pastry and reaching out reflexively to steady her. My hand landed on her hip.

I was trying to stay focused, but her hip was a nice soft curve and my fingers sank into it.

"You okay?" I asked hoarsely.

"I'm good." Her voice was a little breathless.

"Do you have a towel? I am so sorry," I repeated.

Casey straightened and walked around the counter. "It's okay." Her voice was high-pitched. She produced a towel from under the counter and dabbed at her shirt. "Do you want me to make you another coffee?"

"Absolutely not. I still have half of this one. I feel bad leaving now that I spilled most of my coffee on you."

"It's fine," she squeaked.

"You sure?" I asked.

Her auburn ponytail bounced with her nod. "I'll just walk you back to the door."

She held the small white towel in front of her chest as she followed me back toward the door.

"I feel like I should give you more money." I didn't know what else to do at this point.

"Definitely don't do that. You slipped on the floor and spilled some coffee. No big deal."

My wits finally caught up to the situation and I chuckled. I eyed the floor by the door. "Let me clean this up," I offered.

"You really don't need to do that, Leo," Casey said.

Her cheeks were getting pinker by the second. She looked up at me with the towel clutched in one hand and the key in the other. I took the key from her, my fingers brushing hers as I did. The brief touch was like a little bolt of lightning zipping up my arm.

Holy fucking hell, Casey was too cute. It wasn't rational, but I came by for coffee all the time just to get a glimpse of her. There were lots of reasons why I shouldn't be doing that.

I kept a firm grip on my coffee as I opened the door, so I didn't screw this all up all over again. She was waiting with the towel still clutched in front of her.

"I owe you one," I said.

She paused for a minute and then nodded. "You kinda do."

I chuckled. "I'm glad you agree. What should I do?"

She cocked her head to the side, seeming to have found her composure as she looked up at me. A teasing glint entered her gaze. "I'm gonna have to think on that. I was closing when you came in. I could've told you we were done for the day. And then..." She waved the towel up and down in front of her chest. "I'll think of the right price."

I burst out laughing, and when she giggled in response, lust revved its engine. It was like a little kick, a jumpstart in my body. For a mess of reasons, my body had been pretty shut down lately.

"Well, you know I'll be seeing you around. Just let me know what I can do. And, thank you again."

After I left, Casey locked the door behind me. As I walked away, I realized I was actually looking forward to something. I hadn't looked forward to anything in too damned long.

. . .

Thank you for reading Stella & Hudson's story! Want a glimpse of the future for them? Join my newsletter to receive an exclusive scene.

Sign up here: https://BookHip.com/KQWVWNS

p.s. If you are already subscribed, you'll still be able to access the scene.

Up next is in the Wild Fire Series is Fake It True.

How we met: He spilled coffee on me.
First date: I dragged him into a therapy session. Does that count as a date?
Spoiler alert: We're not a couple.

I *know* it sounds ridiculous, but I needed someone to pretend to be my fiancé. When I collide with Leo Massie in the waiting room at my therapist's office, I drag him in with me.

Next thing I know, we're fake engaged and I'm in over my head and my hormones are having a field day over Leo. Maybe it's funny at first, but Leo is protecting me from something very real, and my heart is getting in on the action.

Don't miss Casey & Leo's emotional, protective and swoony romance!

One-click: Fake It True - due out April 2025!

For more swoon & sass...

This Crazy Love kicks off the Swoon Series - small town southern romance with enough heat to melt you! Jackson & Shay's story is epic - swoon-worthy & intensely emotional. Jackson just happens to be Shay's brother's best friend. He's also *seriously* easy on the eyes. Shay has a past, the kind of past she would most definitely like to forget. Past or not, Jackson is about to rock her world. Don't miss their story!

Burn For Me is a second chance romance for the ages. Sexy firefighters? Check. Rugged men? Check. Wrapped up together? Check. Brave the fire in this hot, small-town romance. Amelia & Cade were high school sweethearts & then it all fell apart. When they cross paths again, it's epic - don't miss Cade's story!

For more small town romance, take a visit to Last Frontier Lodge in Diamond Creek. A sexy, alpha SEAL meets his match with a brainy heroine in Take Me Home. Marley is all brains & Gage is all brawn. Sparks fly when their worlds collide. Don't miss Gage & Marley's story!

If sports romance lights your spark, check out The Play. Liam is a British footballer who falls for Olivia, his doctor. A twist of forbidden heats up this swoon-worthy & laugh-out-loud romance. Don't miss Liam & Olivia's story.

Be sure to sign up for my newsletter for the latest news, teasers & more! Click here to sign up: http://jhcroixauthor.com/subscribe/

ACKNOWLEDGMENTS

A shout of thanks to my readers! This author life can be so lonely sometimes. More often than I'd like to admit, I wonder if my books are worth reading. Then, along comes a reader who sends me a note to tell me they love a story. Trust me when I say those notes matter to authors. *A lot.*

To my editor, Virginia Tesi Carey, who keeps steering these characters and story along the way. My proofreader is still correcting me when I mess up on the details. My early readers keep me on my toes and make sure the stubborn errors are fixed. Anything left is simply there to remind me I will never be perfect.

Najla Qamber has created the gorgeous covers for this series and is so gracious and kind. Erin, my assistant, is the organization behind my author life and helps me in so many ways. Bless you, Erin!

To my hubs, my family, and my dogs. All my love.
xoxo
J.H. Croix

FIND MY BOOKS

Thank you for reading When We Dare! I hope you enjoyed the story. If so, you can help other readers find my books in a variety of ways.

1) Write a review!
2) Sign up for my newsletter, so you can receive information about upcoming new releases & receive a FREE copy of one of my books: http://jhcroixauthor.com/subscribe/
3) Like and follow my Amazon Author page at https://amazon.com/author/jhcroix
4) Follow me on Bookbub at https://www.bookbub.com/authors/j-h-croix
5) Follow me on Instagram at https://www.instagram.com/jhcroix/

6) Like my Facebook page at https://www.facebook.com/jhcroix

Wild Fire Series
All The Afters
When We Dare
Fake It True - due out April 2025!
Only Ever You - coming soon!
Fireweed Harbor Series
Make You Mine
Dare To Fall
Be The One
One More Time
Wait For You
Ever After All
Light My Fire Series
Wild With You
Hold Me Now
Only Ever Us
Fall For Me
Keep Me Close
With Every Breath
All It Takes
Take Me Now
Meant To Be
Dare With Me Series
Crash Into You

Evers & Afters
Come To Me
Back To Us
Take Me There
After We Fall
Swoon Series
This Crazy Love
Wait For Me
Break My Fall
Truly Madly Mine
Still Go Crazy
If We Dare
Steal My Heart
Into The Fire Series
Burn For Me
Slow Burn
Burn So Bad
Hot Mess
Burn So Good
Sweet Fire
Play With Fire
Melt With You
Burn For You
Crash & Burn
That Snowy Night
Haven's Bay Holiday Series
All I Want
All I Need
All We Have

All We Are
Brit Boys Sports Romance
The Play
Big Win
Out Of Bounds
Play Me
Naughty Wish
Diamond Creek Alaska Novels
When Love Comes
Follow Love
Love Unbroken
Love Untamed
Tumble Into Love
Christmas Nights
Lodge Series
Take Me Home
Love at Last
Just This Once
Falling Fast
Stay With Me
When We Fall
Hold Me Close
Crazy For You
Just Us

ABOUT THE AUTHOR

USA Today Bestselling Author J. H. Croix lives in a small town with her husband and just one spoiled dog. Croix writes contemporary romance with sassy women and alpha men who aren't afraid to show some emotion. Her love for quirky small-towns and the characters that inhabit them shines through in her writing. When she's not writing, you can find her cooking, counting the birds in her backyard, and running with her dog, which is when her best plotting happens.

Places you can find me:
jhcroixauthor.com
jhcroix@jhcroix.com

facebook.com/jhcroix
instagram.com/jhcroix
bookbub.com/authors/j-h-croix